THE TRUE STORY OF THE VICE QUEEN

I wish to thank the following, who helped me to save my life: my daughter Catherine; Coolmine Therapeutic Community; my friend Stephen. A special thanks to Marino Books, especially to Jo O'Donoghue, who put so much of her energy into helping me to write this book.

THE TRUE STORY OF THE VICE QUEEN

MARESE O'SHEA

First published in 1997 by
Marino Books
16 Hume Street Dublin 2
Trade enquiries to CMD Distribution
55A Spruce Avenue Stillorgan Industrial
Park Blackrock County Dublin

© Marese O'Shea 1997

ISBN 1 86023 055 5

10 9 8 7 6 5 4 3 2 1

A CIP record for this title is available
from the British Library

Cover photograph courtesy of the
Sunday World
Cover design by Penhouse Design
Set by Richard Parfrey
Printed in Ireland by ColourBooks,
Baldoyle Industrial Estate, Dublin 13

This book is dedicated to the memory of my father,
my mother and my brother Damien

CONTENTS

CHRONOLOGY

1960   Marese O'Shea (Louise Finn) born
1975   Louise's adoptive father dies
1976   Spends summer in psychiatric hospital
1978   Catherine, Louise's daughter, born
1978   Louise's first customer in Mount Street
1979   Begins to work in massage parlour in Thomas Street
1981   Undergoes surgery for gynaecological problems; Damien, Louise's brother, dies in France
1983   First trip to America
1984–6 'Works' Waterloo Road as well as parlours
1986   Becomes very successful; rents apartment in Clanwilliam Court
1990   Sets up Euro-Escorts, also known as Exclusive Escorts
1991   Provides 'toyboy' service; 'Goodtime Girls Go Nationwide'; exclusive Christmas parties. Also traces biological mother and meets cousin
1992   Marese O'Shea Bureau
1994   Louise's first stay in Coolmine
1994–5 Louise back working the street (Fitzwilliam Square)
1995–6 Second stay in Coolmine
1996   Louise's mother dies of cancer; Louise begins to write *The True Story of the Vice Queen*

1

CHILDHOOD

I was adopted, and my earliest recollection is of when I was seven. There was something wrong in the house and I knew it. My mother gave me two in one: 'Your father is dying and you are adopted' in the one sentence. She left it at that but I constantly went over it in my mind. My father – my adoptive father, although I didn't understand what that meant – went blind when I was seven; he had diabetes. I had a brother, Damien, who is dead; he drowned about fifteen years ago. Damien was three years younger than me. He was not my blood brother but adopted as well. We went to private schools as the family was comfortably off financially. My father had been in a good managerial job in Posts and Telegraphs in the GPO so we lived in a nice house and had a good standard of living. At this stage of my life we lived in Dundrum. When the diabetes caused my father to become completely blind my mother had to work – she ran a Montessori school. My mother had to keep up our standard of living. I'd come home from school and look after my brother and my father. From the age of seven on.

People often find it strange that I have no memories earlier than seven. In fact I do have one recollection – all my memories seem to be of awful things – of when I found my grandfather dead in bed when I was three, three and a half. He was living with us. He was my adoptive mother's father and I was very, very close to him. I remember him coming in the door and giving me shiny pennies and grapes with glucose on them. He used to spoil me with bars of chocolate. I ran up one morning to wake him up but I didn't know he was dead. I knew there was some thing wrong and then, of course, there was panic. I think he was maybe in his seventies.

I don't have very many memories of school. I can vaguely recall crying on the first day I went there. I do remember my first communion and I think I was only six when I made it. The earliest memory that has any meaning is of my father being ill and my mother telling me at the kitchen table. No, actually she was standing at the cooker and she just said it to me: 'Your Dad is very sick; he is dying.' By then he had been told as well. The diabetes had just gone too far. He was very young when he died – in his early fifties. At the time I'm talking about he would have been only in his forties.

When I was in Coolmine undergoing drug rehabilitation therapy I remembered back to three and a half and finding my grandfather dead. I had forgotten all about my grandfather and to this day I would have said that around seven is my earliest recollection if it hadn't been that Coolmine jogged my memory. I really don't have any memories of being a child. I know I never went out to play with other children because we were very protected in that way; it was always just with family.

My mother wasn't affectionate but she wasn't severe either. She was just so caught up in her own world, so worried knowing that my father was going to die and that she had two young children to rear. She had had a tough life herself. Growing up I was very bitter towards her but now I feel a lot of guilt about the way I treated her. I blamed her for my life, for my problems. I blamed her for my biological mother putting me up for adoption. I blamed her for everything. She put a lot of value on money instead of feelings. I never felt she loved me as a person but she acted in the best way she could. In her head she believed she loved me. I don't think she really knew what love was. She definitely didn't love herself.

She would buy you the world but she just didn't know how to give you physical affection. She really wasn't ready for children; I mean ready emotionally. She couldn't have children of her own. She and my father tried, and I think at one stage she had a miscarriage. Then they obviously decided to adopt.

I remember one time when I stole something as a child of about seven or eight, along with other children out of school. We thought this was great, stealing things like markers out of the local H. Williams. Of course I got caught, and I deserved it. I went to my mother, terrified. I thought it was the end of the world. I kept saying: 'I'm sorry, Ma,' and she said, 'Get away from me'. At the time I really needed her and she just didn't have a clue.

My father was completely different; I was like glue to him. He was my world; I idolised him. He was gentle, funny, kind, intelligent and affectionate, and I trusted him a hundred per cent. In the seven years until he died, when I was nearly fourteen, I had this amazing bond with him because he was blind. I became his eyes and when he died I was lost.

I went to Notre Dame des Missions school. I went there to secondary school as well and I remember the walk home. We used to live up in Meadowmount and there was a big hill from Notre Dame up home. I used to walk with a girl from across the road who used to boss me – kick me up the hill literally. Since my Da was blind he couldn't bring me home and my mother had to work. The girl was just messing around, making me do things, making me touch her.

I was very confused when I found out I was adopted, although I knew that another girl in my class was adopted too. I was told that my natural parents didn't want me. I didn't really understand this and was so confused I just became a wreck. I must have spoken to somebody about it because I did realise that I couldn't find my mother until I was eighteen. I couldn't do anything about it but I always knew from a very young age, even twelve, that I wanted to find her. Why, I don't know, because at that stage my adoptive mother and my father were there. I just wanted to know who she was. I think it's a very natural thing to want to know. I'd always heard people saying to others: 'Oh the baby looks like you,' but I didn't have anybody that I looked like.

Because my father was so sick and had to have operations, members of his family came home to see him. One of his relatives abused me. We were alone in the house but he knew that my mother never stayed out for long; he pulled me in behind the fridge so if anyone came in they wouldn't have seen me.

I knew that what he was doing was wrong; I hated him for it and was really angry but I didn't do anything or tell anybody. I later had reason to think that he abused my brother as well. This went on until I was about fourteen or fifteen but from then on I avoided him. After my father died, I was only once in his company and even then he was looking at me that way. I made sure that I always stayed with other people, that I wasn't on my own with him, because I was frightened of the power he had over me.

He would make me touch him as he was touching me and when sometimes he came off I was terrified. It was the most frightening thing ever. I remember a couple of times I thought he was dying or I didn't know what. I'll never forget it. Then he'd pull up his clothes and put money on the table, usually a pound or two. And he always gave me money in an envelope at Christmas. For that reason my mother thought he was very good to me.

My mother was always anxious about me, put me in a glass case, locked me away. I suppose her anxiety had to do with our being adopted. She was so protective that it was damaging. It meant that other children of my own age played no part in my life. I may have been allowed to school a number of hours a day but that was it. I was never allowed out. I used to go to my aunt's on the Navan Road for the weekend. The freedom, being let out to play! She was my mother's sister and she was brilliant, a perfect person for a mother. She's still alive but unfortunately living with cancer now. She's a wonderful person. My cousins were much older, the youngest about fifteen years older than me, but I had loads of people to play with there and I made a friend next door I could go out with.

By the time I was in my early teens I used to go off and drink. My mates were schoolgirls from Churchtown and some from the Navan Road. We'd go to the Wesley and Bective Rangers clubhouse, especially when there was a disco. We put make-up on and got dressed up. Sometimes we'd steal the alcohol out of friends' houses.

At around this time I was aware that my father was getting sicker. He was still at home but he had to go to hospital a lot, in and out. I'd come home from school and find an ambulance there. The fear every day that I'd come home and he might be gone was very severe. I suppose I drank because I was so miserable and hated myself so much. I just hadn't coped at all with my Dad's illness. If he hadn't been so sick I might have been able to ask him for help. He died in hospital. I had been in that night to see him. I remember I had new shoes and I was 'showing' them to him – I used to describe things to him. He was so sick he couldn't hold anything down. I remember being frightened because he kept getting sick. He died later on that night, after I had left the hospital. It was better for him but it was shocking for me. It reminded me of when I was eight. My mother's brother Joe and his wife Vera lived next door to us in Dundrum. I was very close to Joe and spent a lot of time in his house. He was the first to introduce me to classical music. I remember him being sick at home and visiting him in the Richmond Hospital where they were treating him for cancer.

I had managed to prevent anyone finding out about

my drinking while I was at school. I liked school and I liked studying, which probably sounds strange, but I liked to do well. But there was so much happening at home, sickness and stuff. There was never any stability in the household that I can remember. I didn't deal at all well with the death. I just felt a great loss of comfort and safety. I hadn't even thought to prepare myself.

I talked to no one but went off and lived my own life. I showed no signs of grief. My mother was very upset but she had so much on her plate that she just had to get on with it. She had to get on with bringing the money in for private education. I was to go on a school trip to Europe and she provided the cash. She kept her house; she was very determined to have the best of material things. She did get a bit of a pension but she was always a spender and tended to live beyond her means. I ended up paying for it. I was already earning at that age. I started baby-sitting when I was thirteen and I'd usually have a few bob to spend.

Then I was caught with drink at school when I was still only fifteen. My friend and I had mixed a little bottle made out of a lot of different kinds of alcohol. We'd stolen it from her house. That day she brought the bottle and we went off to the hockey shed. I had some tablets, Valium or something. I don't know where I got them. While I was taking them we were caught by one of the nuns. We were hauled up and the doctor was called in and a psychologist. That was a year after my father died. The psychologist said that I needed a rest. I went home drunk another night that week and there were records there and I was so upset I began to smash them and throw them on the fire to burn. That's all I was doing. I was on my own; I wasn't near anybody or violent to anybody.

The doctors were called and they put me into St Loman's. I had a relative who was a chaplain there, and he thought I should go there first but that was heavy. There was nothing wrong with me; I was only wild. The whole idea was crazy; I was actually abused there by one of the patients. I was only a kid and I didn't need to be locked up. I wasn't even aware of the drugs that they were giving me.

They transferred me to St John of God's after a couple of nights. That was a nightmare as well. An absolutely horrifying situation for a fifteen-year-old. They pumped me with drugs and I had never really taken drugs. We weren't into drugs at all; what we were doing was drinking. But I came out of there addicted to Largactil, an anti-depressant. They used to inject it into me at the time and the dose lasted twenty-four hours. Sometimes they would dose me repeatedly for a week at a time.

As far as I remember it was June of 1976 when they took me into St John of God's. I was going to be sixteen in October. It was a fabulous summer, I recall. I was locked up in a room but I could see my friends walking up the drive and hear them outside my door. But they wouldn't let them see me. Then if I got noisy they'd end up injecting me and knocking me out for days.

My problem was that I was angry all the time. I was put in a locked ward, instead of getting the doctor or a counsellor. There was no real psychiatric help. The shrink would look at you, show you a stupid picture and ask: 'What do you think of this?' It was all nonsense; they should have had the guts to say, 'You can't behave like this!'

When I got out I was in a dreadful state. I was registered as an alcoholic at fifteen while I was in John of God's. I was a hundred times worse than when I went in. I was addicted to sleeping pills. I came out of there an emotional mess; my head was so fucked up. I was glad to get out, and fair play to my mother she did sign me out when she realised that it was doing me nothing but harm. She had signed me in so there was no problem about release. There was no problem either about getting more pills. I was on pills of one kind or another until I was twenty-two.

2

SALESWOMAN AND MOTHER

I went back to school for as long as it took to do the Inter Cert but I left when I was sixteen. I didn't know what I wanted to do. At that time one of the done things when you left school was to go and do a secretarial course so I did that. I started working in offices and eventually I became a saleswoman. That suited me well. I was never a day without work and then it went brilliantly saleswise. In the office jobs I would meet salespeople and I used to say to them, give me a go. I began making a good living selling on commission. Soon I was running a chain of butcher's shops.

I could have stayed there and made a lot of money because I had a genuine ability as a salesperson and was smart with accounts. When the owner went abroad for a year he left me to handle everything. I had to sell the meat, beg the wholesalers to keep up the supply and get in the money from outstanding accounts. I worked very hard for a whole year and it took an awful lot out of me. At the end of the day all the work was for somebody else – it wasn't mine. When the owner came back I said goodbye. We stayed friends and I'm glad we did.

After that I went to work in Mount Carmel hospital. It might seems strange that I should work in a hospital after my experiences in John of God's. Yet I have always loved medical stuff. At home I had medical encyclopaedias. I really should have pursued a career in medicine. I wouldn't have fancied being a nurse, though; I would have had to be a doctor. That's why I didn't look for work as a nurse's aide. I went into the radiology department because someone was out temporarily; unfortunately when they came back I had no job. The pay in Mount Carmel was very poor. I couldn't live on the money I was earning there compared to what I was getting in sales so I was still working as a saleswoman part-time, at night. I did all kinds of work. I had got to know other butchers and some of them used to ring me to ask me to do work for them. I did typing for companies at night. I've sold everything: houses, cars, you name it, I've sold it. I suppose prosti-tution is a kind of selling. In it as in everything else, you'll not succeed unless you have faith in what you're selling. If someone came to me with something that was bogus, I couldn't sell it.

After I left the hospital I was working for an alumin-ium firm in Churchtown, a Bristol company. I was selling for them, aluminium windows and doors, and I was also running their office in Dublin. I had been over to Bristol to see their operation. Then they bought a big factory in Tallaght and they wanted me to move out but it was too far from Churchtown to get to Tallaght every day, so I left that job.

At this stage I wasn't sleeping around but I had been

with a couple of guys. I wasn't a virgin but I wasn't promiscuous either. I don't exactly remember when I lost my virginity. I must have been about sixteen. I had my daughter when I was nearly eighteen and I didn't get pregnant with her the first time I had sex. My daughter was born when I was still working for the aluminium company and I went back to work three weeks after I had her. The father was, I suppose, a childhood sweetheart. He was OK, only a kid. We were having sex for nine months with no protection. Every month I'd be thinking, oh, I didn't get my period. It was inevitable it was going to happen even though I kept thinking, ah no it won't, the age-old story, it won't happen to me. Well it did. I stopped drinking then. When I was expecting my baby I didn't drink at all.

It never occurred to me to have an abortion, never. I was still living at home. I was six months pregnant before I went to a doctor or told my mother. I was beginning to show and one day she said to me, 'You're getting a terrible stomach! Are you pregnant?' That was my opportunity but I didn't say anything just then. I went to Cherish. The people there suggested to me that I could go down the country to Cork or somewhere till I had the baby and come back up then. But I didn't.

I mentioned that possibility to my mother when I told her. I said, 'Look, I'm pregnant.' She said, 'You're staying here,' which was probably the worst thing I could have done because she used my daughter against me ever after. So instead of going to Cork, the next day we were out buying nappies and that night she rang her doctor to get the name of a gynaecologist and that was it. She took it well, maybe because she had never been pregnant herself. Before I knew it she was saying, 'You're going to a private doctor in Fitzwilliam Square.'

I carried on at work. In spite of the social attitudes of the time my mother was very calm. I felt any disgrace more than she did. I decided, too, that there would be no contact with the father; that was a deliberate thing. I knew that I was very young and I wasn't going to marry him so it was better that there was no connection. As far as I was concerned, it was just me and my daughter. He knew about the pregnancy but he was glad not to be blamed. He was young too, and I suppose he was glad that he wouldn't get into trouble. I did not encourage him to take any part and naturally enough he made no attempt to see me after the baby was born. I was thinking of being tied, I suppose. I denied Catherine her rights but I think my playing of it suited him as well. She knows who her father is but there's no acquaintance. He married and had kids but he and his wife are separated.

I worked and had the baby, and I wasn't unhappy about it. Maybe the fact that I was adopted made me want to keep my child. I don't believe there's any reason in the world to give away your baby if society will feed you and look after you. I know some people aren't capable of managing but you can't say that every child that's adopted will be happier than the ones kept by a single parent. They might be a mess if you keep them but they might be a mess if you give them away as well. It depends on who they are adopted by. I think that it's better when the child stays with the mother, even a single mother, as long as she is fit to be a mother.

Catherine was born in Holles Street and it wasn't a very difficult birth, although it did go to a forceps delivery. And I loved her and now treasure her all the more because I can't have any more children. She is just a gift to me. Though I was only eighteen I knew what a gift she was. I was very lucky, too: my mother ran the Montessori school in our house so there were always loads of children. She was able to look after Catherine when I was out working. I was there in the evening. My brother loved her as well. It was fine at the start. I was happy that my mother was looking after my daughter until she started to use her against me.

I suppose she began to think that she had some sort of right to Catherine, almost as if she were her own child. In the end she actually made her claim, not legally, but by God she did want to take her away from me. She deliberately turned her against me as a person, telling her I was no good. It was a bit like the way she behaved to me, telling me things about my own birth mother that were totally untrue.

3
—

THE MAN IN MOUNT STREET

Catherine was born in July 1978. I was eighteen the following October. My mother gave me a car for my eighteenth birthday and that was how I got into trouble financially. She paid the deposit and I made the repayments. The insurance was £1,000.

I was in the aluminium company, doing sales. The money was quite good but it wasn't enough to cover my expenses as regards the insurance, tax, petrol to keep the car going. I decided that I needed some way of earning money. I remember talking to a taxi driver I knew. I was sitting in his car and I said to him, 'I don't know what I'm going to do for money; I can't live on the money I have.' He said: 'Sure, go to one of these massage parlours and you'd get £5 for topless and £10 for a strip.' I kept his advice in mind. I wouldn't say I was promiscuous at that stage and I did have reservations, but after hearing that I considered it seriously.

One night I was out with a friend. We were around Baggot Street and driving by the Pepper Canister church when this car pulled up beside me. The driver was looking over and signalling for us to stop. I was quite naïve at the time; I think I knew it was a red light district but I didn't have prostitution in my head at that stage. He was youngish and attractive and I did stop. He was really quite nice and I had no money for petrol. I was desperate for money so I suppose I must have intentionally gone there, driven around that area just to see what might transpire. I didn't have sex with him and all I got was £10.

I've often thought about that first customer. I parked my car and went off with him. We didn't go far. I was terrified, not so much of him, but of the other girls who were prostitutes. I was afraid that they would attack me because I'd heard rumours about prostitution at that stage which were totally unfounded. You know the sort of thing: all prostitutes are bad; the girls are rough and ready. I was afraid of the unknown as well. I didn't even know how much to charge. He asked me for sex and I said, 'I don't do sex.' He said, 'You're not a normal prostitute; you're not normally down here.' I suppose I wasn't dressed like the others: no fake leopard skin or the rest.

I was dressed then as I always dressed later when I was working; I always wore beautiful suits and stockings. I never stood out on the street; I never stopped. I always walked, so that if someone I knew saw me it looked like I was on my way home from work. I was always dressed like a businesswoman with stockings and that – white stockings and white gloves. I think that my appearance was a turn-on.

It was fairly obvious that the guy was a regular. I can't be absolutely certain but I'd say he was; he knew the story. But then a lot of men are – the majority. I think it's an addiction. I had no sense of disgust myself; it was just something I did for ten quid. I told Philomena all about it and she wasn't a bit upset either. She was the friend who later came with me to Thomas Street. She wasn't easily shocked. She slept around a lot but didn't do anything for money. I needed the money and she knew it. That was that. It was all very quick – only five minutes, I'd say, in the car. At that stage I hadn't done sex so I didn't really know what it entailed.

I suppose it must seem strange; here was I with a baby only a few months old, giving a stranger hand relief. The fact was I hadn't got a penny in my pocket, my car needed petrol and I had bills to pay. I was broke because I had spent any money I had on alcohol. I used to go out at weekends drinking with my friends, during the week as well. I remember dying of a hangover in work during the week with my head down on the desk. It wasn't really accidental that I was in there in a place I knew was a red light district. But I was green, totally. I hadn't even read stories about prostitution when I went along there. I took the opportunity, earned my ten pounds and that got me by.

I continued in the straight job for about a year after that but the financial pressures got worse and worse. I decided I needed to make a strong decision. I remember that it was then I made up my mind to go into prostitution. I had thought about it for most of that year, all the pros and cons. The person, the taxi-man who had recommended that I go into it, was very intelligent. I idolised him and believed everything he said. He was much older than me, like a father-figure, although it may seem to be strange advice to have given to a young girl. Somebody else might have urged me to go back to school, do the Leaving and try for third-level education. Or say I should stick with the aluminium company and make a career there. But he didn't. He may have been cynical but he probably knew that it was the most likely career for one with my temperament and in my situation.

It is very hard to know why people do things. Maybe he secretly wished to be the one who knew that I worked as a prostitute to earn fast money and that it was on his advice. He was an interesting man; he'd been to university. It was his choice to drive a taxi. That's why I believed him and took his advice. At the time I didn't go too deeply into his motives. Maybe it was only a joke that I took too seriously. I myself certainly wouldn't give that advice to anybody. I probably paid more attention to his advice than I should have because no one in my family offered to help me.

It helped, I suppose, that I had no regular boyfriend. I had split up with my daughter's father. I did have a relationship for a while with a guy. I'd really fallen for him but then one day he turned around and said, 'I'm in love with my secretary,' so that was that. I was broken up a bit at the end of it. Maybe this too had some influence on my decision – all the circumstances at the time seemed to lead to that decision.

On the positive side I was able to give my mother a regular income from my work in the aluminium company and she was happy enough. I was home every evening and bonding well with Catherine. After the aluminium company moved to Tallaght, I worked for a while with a telephone company but I couldn't content myself with my job there. I was drinking a lot and the money was poor so it didn't make sense to me. That influenced me too; everything influenced me to give prostitution a try.

4
—

THOMAS STREET

When I decided on prostitution I went to Thomas Street.
I found the name of a massage parlour in a magazine. I
knew nothing about the game, didn't know any prostitutes. I rang and they said can you come in for an
interview today and I was delighted. I asked my friend
Philomena to come with me. All dressed up in whatever
fashion was around for eighteen-year-olds, I drove to
Thomas Street and parked right outside the door. The
business was on the first and second floors. I looked up
and I saw the blinds drawn. I noticed that they were
Venetian blinds.

The place was over a shop and the sign on the door
said Embassy but it was known by the street number. I
said to my friend, 'If I'm not out in ten minutes, come
and get me.' I was so green I thought I was going to be
held in there and not let out. I really didn't know anything. Still I went in and up the stairs. The door was
locked. One of the girls answered my knock. She was quite
scantily dressed and very good-looking with long dark
hair. I was taken into a little room which was cosy and

warm, with a nice carpet. It wasn't a bad place; a bit seedy but quite comfortable. The boss was there, a funny character.

I hadn't worked before, so I thought it might be a problem getting a job. No sex allowed, this was what they used to say, what they'd tell you at the interview; they had to cover themselves. But there *was* sex. I was told topless for a fiver, strip for a tenner, Swedish massage for fifteen. I didn't know what a Swedish massage was but I soon heard, in plain English. I thought it would be impossible because I'm very small. Swedish massage is like hand relief except that instead of using your hand you use your breasts. I was told it was £20 for a reverse massage, where I'd lie up on the table and get a massage.

I said OK, they said start tomorrow; so I did. I lied at home when I said I was going into work. The place opened at ten in the morning and there were two shifts: ten till five and five till eleven. The other girl was there, the girl I had met the day before, and a customer came in. She said, 'Do you want to do him?' I was terrified. I didn't know what to do. I went out and I opened the door and took this guy in. I still remember who he was.

We used whatever room was free; there were three altogether, of different sizes. One of the small rooms was got up like a massage parlour, with a couch.

My first guy was a very big businessman whom I didn't know then, though I got to know him later. He was always a good tipper. The system worked like this: there was an entrance fee of £12 but that went to the management so you were completely dependent on what the customer would tip you. If you didn't get your tip you'd be doing it for nothing. They didn't always tip. Apparently a hand relief was supposed to be included in the twelve. It was something I would never allow, on principle. They'd say, well if you're going to work here you'll do it. I'd say, well then I won't work here. They knew that I had very regular customers, so they would lose by my leaving.

The customer was supposed to give you five for topless and ten for a strip. What would regularly happen was that the customer would give twelve at the door and say, 'I don't want any extras, just the hand relief.' I would say, 'No; you have one of the extras.' I would never give them the hand relief unless they paid for one of the extras. Some girls would and this always made me angry.

Anyway: the first customer was asking for sex. First he put £200 cash on the table, saying, 'There you go.' I was saying no, no, no because I thought you weren't allowed to do sex; I found out later that you were. Then it came to the crucial part of it and I didn't know what to do. The actual sexual relief part. I had done hand relief once with the man in Mount Street but that wasn't really the same. The guy in Mount Street wasn't stripped, this guy was. I didn't even know how to handle a man.

The other girl showed me; she came in and did it in front of me. I knew from then on what to do. I learnt the tricks of the trade. I felt my way at first. Massage and so on. That was my first customer. I think I got £15 from him for going topless. He was a good tipper; he gave the other girl £30 and she shared it with me.

For my first two weeks I didn't do sex. I was green but I made £90 on topless on my first day. Within two weeks I was doing sex because everyone was. The customer would say, 'But I did it with that other girl.' There was a 'two-girl' one day; he wanted sex with two girls at the one time. You'd usually get around £30 a go for sex, but you'd always have the cheapskates as well.

There was this girl in the massage parlour who was much older than me. She must have been about fifteen years older and she was a real bitch, not very popular. There was a lot of jealousy between the girls. If you were popular with a customer they'd say, well you must be doing things without protection. All this instead of just saying fair play to you. A paying man is anybody's. So this older one would say to me, 'You should go and work in the Bay Tree,' because she wanted to get rid of me. I started getting the same guys coming back. I was new and young but even if I hadn't been young, it was enough that I was new. For a lot of guys meeting a different person every time is their thing. But you do get regulars: I have a guy now whom I've been seeing for years. I don't mind it when a customer wants to try somebody else. That's their privilege. Actually I like them to because there's a lot of pressure on you if you get attached to a customer. Every week you'd be dreading the regulars coming in again. I used to say to them, 'Why don't you go to X or Y?' to give myself a break.

I used to do lessons as well. Some guys would bring their girls in with them. I would totally recommend this and I still do to this day, especially for married couples. There are so many things that can be done, that people can learn. There was a guy who used to bring in his girlfriend and he would have me touching her with him. I would never have sex with the guy while the girlfriend was there but some would. It's not as if the girl would just be watching; she would be joining in.

I became successful and popular and once I started doing sex I was earning as much as £300 a day. Of course I took all the necessary precautions: I always insisted on the customers using a condom. It was protection not only against becoming pregnant but also against disease. Syphilis and gonorrhea, in those days. I even protected my skin, putting on lotion to avoid getting scabies or pubic lice. Sometimes I would even make customers use condoms for hand relief.

At home I pretended I was selling make-up and that sort of thing. It was the excuse many of the girls used for their friends and family. It covers you at the start. I wasn't all that keen on Thomas Street. It was a rough area and one of the girls was attacked. The standard of hygiene wasn't great either. The towels weren't clean or anything so I always used my own. The girl who was jealous and trying to get rid of me kept on saying, 'You should go and work at the Bay Tree; you'd be very busy there.' I'd heard it was a better class of place so I decided to check it out.

It was located over in Rathmines/Portobello. I was about twenty at the time, which would make it about 1980. I had only been in Thomas Street for a couple of months when I left. I would probably have been better off staying where I was but anyway I went. Bay Tree was a house with steps down into a courtyard. It was beautiful, an end house, and really luxurious, I have to give it that. Beautiful carpets, couches, bedrooms, VIP room. The thing was, the guy who was running it was a woman-hater. His mouth was just filthy and that's what you had to put up with. But the money was fantastic. I was making hundreds of pounds a day. This meant handling about ten customers. They were mostly well off and there were quite a few VIPs among them. Bay Tree had the name of being the best.

Every time you came out of the room you had to write down how much the customer gave you. The admission charge was from £15 to £25 – the top of the range was for a VIP – and the customer paid you separately for whatever you did for him.

It was a two-storey house. Upstairs there were two massage rooms; downstairs a lounge where all the girls would sit and the customers would choose who they wanted. Across the hall was the VIP room, which included a large round corner bath, luxurious furniture and carpet and a vibrating bed for massage. Customers would ask you to join them in the bath and you'd wash and pamper them, dry them and oil them. You'd be guaranteed a minimum of £30 to £50 for this. I was shining clean in the Bay Tree because I lived in the VIP bath.

One day the owner took me into the VIP room. The place was quiet and he put a note on the door saying 'Call back.' I was terrified, dreading what might happen. I'd heard he did that, took the girls into the room on his own. So he said to me, 'Run the bath, Lisa.' I knew what was going to happen but he turned out to be really nice, a real gentleman. I got on well with him. I was very surprised because I had the impression that he was a woman-hater. After we finished he put £50 in my pocket. I liked that too. I always like my customers to put my money into an envelope rather than hand it to me. The gentlemen always did.

The rule at the Bay Tree that you had to write down what the customer gave you got me into real difficulties and meant the end of my job. The owner was in trouble with the law. The place was raided by the guards; it had been broken into and smashed up and I was told not to come in the next day, which I didn't. Then the guards (who had got all the files) called me at one o'clock in the morning. I was in bed in Churchtown and they brought me down to the station in Kevin Street. Of course they all had big smiles because they knew exactly how many customers there were – everything. They asked me about the owner and I told them what I knew. They had all the evidence anyway but I went and signed a statement, not realising what was going to happen. It turned out that I was called as state witness.

The guards didn't usually bother parlours but this particular guy was trouble. It wasn't just the parlour; there were other illegal things as well. Next thing I got a summons to appear in court. I had been so naïve. That was the end of it for me – the worry of it. That place was finished and the owner asked me would I go to the other place he had in Stephen Street, called the Ambassador. I went there for a couple of shifts, then we heard that it was going to be raided too. So I left him altogether and I lived for a while on the money I had made.

The publicity meant that everybody, my mother included, knew what I'd been doing. My name and address were in the paper. At the time we were getting terrible abusive calls and my mother was also getting calls from the owner and people at the parlour threatening what would happen if I went to court. But there was no way out of it. I went to a solicitor, a very reputable solicitor, and he said to me: as a friend I'd say leave the country, as a solicitor I'd say go to court. When I did I was ripped apart by the defence barrister. In his defence of the owner, he made out that I was the only and that the place wasn't a brothel, although three other women had been caught in the same situation. Although the owner was a bad character I liked him. I made it up with him afterwards.

When I went to Thomas Street I had stopped using my own name; I called myself Lisa at first. I never used my own name as a prostitute. Very few of the girls did.

People sometimes ask me if I ever got involved with customers. It happened a few times. The first time it happened I had to get out of it quickly enough because the guy turned out to be the biggest conman you could imagine. I still don't know how it happened. Because of the nature of my business, I have had to become a good judge of character. Falling for him was the reason I ended up in New York, but that is for later on in the story. I was blinded because I did find myself attracted to him and not just sexually. I was attracted to his personality. He was charming, and when I think how many men I met, day in and day out, for a male personality to attract me was very rare.

I had one decision to make: I had to keep my own sexual enjoyment outside the work I did. It's a bit like a gynaecologist, I suppose. Women's bodies are his job but they don't turn him on at work. I made a pact with myself. I had heard of a lot of women in my line becoming frigid or lesbian. I wasn't a lesbian and I didn't want to become frigid; I like men and have never disliked them. I promised myself that I would never enjoy myself sexually in work. I was afraid because I knew that it wasn't natural to be in a sexual situation so often, to get pleasure so many times a day. If you were getting pleasure in the everyday job, you would eventually become tired of it: it wouldn't do anything for you any more. So I really had to be very strict with myself and I stuck to my own rules.

I had to learn not to become aroused. I would go to peak but then stop. I would have to draw back from it. Some of the customers were very skilled and they didn't like it when I pulled back. They would offer me extra money to enjoy myself. I was never really into the fake. I'd enjoy what I was doing and they'd know that because of the way I did it, but I never lost the fear of becoming uninterested. I think it is quite unusual for prostitutes to enjoy the act very much but you'll not get many to talk about it. A lot of them are harder types; so many women messed up, coming out of poverty, totally abusing themselves, not using protection, having no control over their lives. I met women who were having babies and they didn't even know which customer it was. They'd be saying, 'I hope it isn't Chinese or black.' Sometimes I found it hard to believe what was going on around me.

5
—

Doing Drugs

After the Bay Tree was raided and before the court case
I lived for a while on the money I had made. But before
long I had to go back to work. I was afraid that no other
parlour would take me on because I was going to be seen
in court. Then I got a phone call from one of the girls,
who was working for a guy in Rathmines. He owned two
places and he happened to be a lovely guy. I went to work
in Rathmines in a parlour called the Apollo. The owner
was generous and very kind and for the first time ever
in my experience we got a commission of £3 per customer
– and holiday pay! The drawback was that there was a lot
of drugs in that place. I didn't know that when I started
to work there. I began at the end of the summer and did
my best to block the court case out of my mind. The date
of the case was set for December.

I was in the massage parlour one night and a couple
of the girls were doing heroin. They asked to me if I
wanted to try some. They said it would make me feel
much better. I was obviously in a state and I took it. I was
really vulnerable at the time. I didn't inject, just smoked

it, and that first time I was very sick. The stuff was always available at the parlour and I was there every day at work. If I had come in contact with it socially – just used it once or twice – I might not have become addicted. Once I had started using in the Apollo it was hard for me to avoid it because it was so readily available. One of the girls was only smoking it but others were injecting and of course there were dealers around as well. I was getting quite heavily into it. Some of the girls were addicts so they would have it in the morning and the afternoon. The dealers would be calling in with it and when they'd call you'd get yourself fixed up as soon as a client would give you enough money. At the time they used to sell ten-packs which they now do again. Later the pack went up to quarters. A ten-pack was a small amount, enough for a fix, and a quarter was a quarter of a gramme. This cost £40 at the time although it costs only £10 now.

When I had come out of John of God's five years before, I was addicted to uppers and downers. I kept taking these steadily all during the years in between. I also continued to drink heavily. That's what you want from heroin, to sleep, because you're getting away from everything. So I went on heroin quite easily. I took it not only in the evening but sometimes during the day as well.

The day of the court case in December I was in a pretty bad way. I didn't realise just how bad. The owner of the parlour where I worked came with me to court; he was very kind and supported me all the way through. The morning of the case I arrived early. So I went outside and took heroin. I had a needle with me – at the time some of the girls had needles – and I went into a corner and skin-popped myself with heroin before I went up on the stand. Skin-popping is just to put it into the muscle of the arm or the backside, not trying for a vein. I had skin-popped once before at a party although I have always had a fear of needles. After that I was skin-popping four times a day. Aids wasn't a threat at the time but there were other diseases like hepatitis. That morning I found a space in between two buildings and gave myself the injection there. (It was in Coolmine that that memory of injecting myself came back to me.)

In court the owner got off with a £50 fine. That night after the case I went to a pub. A few of the girls supported me and said, 'Well done!' although it had been horrific. I had one drink in Hughes's pub in Chancery Street, got a taxi and went down to another pub which I knew was the place to buy drugs at the time. It was located down on the quays, way down, towards the North Wall. I had £200 and bought that much worth of heroin, which was twenty ten-packs. When I went out to my taxi a guard stopped me, luckily one I knew. He said, 'You shouldn't be drinking around here.' To my great relief he didn't search me. I went up to Harold's Cross and called to this other dealer I know, took heroin there and bought more off him because I knew the papers were going to come out the next day and I had to stay in. I think I injected that night, not into a vein, just skin-popped again. I overdosed that night. I was unconscious for a while and this guy brought me to.

When I came out of it I just left the house. I was still bad and should have been in hospital. A relative and a friend looked after me. I barely made it. Days were blank; I just don't remember them but I was more or less over it in a week or two. I did it because I knew the papers were coming out and I dreaded the disgrace on my family and myself. Because of the way the case had been handled in court, I was totally destroyed, ripped apart: I just wanted to get away from it all. I knew it was coming but I kept hoping my name wouldn't be in the paper, right up to the very last second. I suppose I should have heeded the solicitor who advised me to get out of Ireland. But my child was here and I wasn't going to leave her. Anyway, I hadn't the money and I was afraid that I would be arrested if I tried to do a bunk.

The news story, which if not the lead was still quite prominent, named the brothel owner who was fined £50 but the whole account was about the girls. As one of the chief witnesses I was named as Louise Finn with an address in Churchtown. The coverage had a lot of lies: stories of my being in a bath with ten men and rubbish like that. My brother was still at school; he was only seventeen at the time and he had to face the disgrace. I still feel very guilty about the misery I caused him.

I didn't see my mother, didn't go home for ages. She moved house then and I couldn't, didn't dare go into the area. What made it worse was that Catherine was with my mother. She was not even three and I couldn't see her. I rang, of course, but every time I did I'd realise that my mother was just devastated and I'd hear the hurt. I couldn't take it; I didn't want to know. And I'd just disappear again. I was drinking very heavily, blocking out all the time.

Then I went back to work at the Apollo at the end of January 1981. I also did shifts in the Lycus in Sackville Place off O'Connell Street, which had the same owner as the Apollo. It was frequented by business people and politicians. It was a pretty low point in my life; I was going on twenty-one, publicly disgraced, and did not see my small daughter for weeks. Still I got through it. I started work again and with the help of my friends tried to get off drugs. I was addicted but I wasn't too far gone at that stage, not to the point I went later on. I stayed away from heroin. I took everything else – sleepers and uppers and cocaine and the rest – but I stayed away from the heroin for more than ten years.

Then the operations started. Before I stopped taking the heroin I was getting pains. They were caused by a low-grade infection caught after Catherine was born. I brought my daughter for her checkup but I didn't bother going for mine. I wasn't even eighteen; I was young and I felt fit again. I went back to work and got my figure back and I didn't bother taking the antibiotics. The infection persisted but I ignored it completely. So the years went by. While I was trying to kick the heroin I stayed with my relatives in Laurel Lodge in Castleknock. There I met Dave, my first love, who is now in America.

We started living together in Castleknock. I had first fancied him when I was eleven or twelve years of age and I met him on and off over the years. I was twenty when we met again and started living together, and the spark was still there. He knew what I did, though he wasn't really into it; he had a full-time job and he was also a musician. He wasn't into heroin so while I was with him I just kept smoking hash and drinking with him. I was working in the Apollo still and I suppose if I hadn't met him I would have ended up killing myself at that stage.

He was my only way out of the gutter. We were mad about each other but because of the mess I was in it turned out to be disastrous. It wouldn't have mattered who I met; I couldn't have got it together because of the state I was in.

One day I was crippled with pain in my stomach. My skin was yellow and I was rolling on the floor in agony. A doctor came and injected me with morphine. He realised that I was addicted and soon he made an arrangement: I'll inject you and you'll look after me sexually. This was happening regularly, a couple of times a week, and I started going into hospital and having operations. Dave stood by me through it all.

I was told I had a growth on my right ovary and the surgeon removed that. I had thought that my womb was out of place after having had my daughter and not going to have my checks. I was very surprised to wake up so ill. I thought it was only going to be a small operation and then I woke up with tubes and drips and machines plugged into the wall and it was very frightening because I was totally on my own, really.

During that year I had a couple of operations and, in between, treatment to cure the infection. Then I had to have another operation because it came back. It wasn't a cancer but a disease that destroyed my whole reproductive system. Not only that but my bladder was in jeopardy, my kidneys, everything in the surrounding area, and even after my womb was removed I was still going for operations. I think I had ten or fifteen of them after that, constantly going in and checking things. Both my ovaries were removed. Eventually I went on hormone treatment and I haven't looked back.

6

—

DAMIEN

My operations continued from January–February of 1981 right through that year. Damien, my brother, went abroad in August after finishing the Leaving Cert. He came into the hospital to say goodbye and he was only two weeks gone when we got a message from the Department of Foreign Affairs that he was missing.

At this stage I was recovering from the operation in the house in Castleknock where I was living with Dave. We used go over to my mother's house in Churchtown every day to see my daughter, or she'd come to us. One day on my way over I stopped at a shop and saw my daughter with a neighbour. Immediately I thought, oh Jesus! I'd better go home. When I arrived I knew immediately: my mother had bad news. Damien's body had been found; he had drowned in a river.

He had been missing for two weeks after having been travelling for about two weeks before that. I didn't know what to do. Though I hadn't been living at home for a while I missed him badly. We'd grown up together. I was never allowed out to play and he was the same; so we only had each other. We had our rows because we only had one television set at the time. (My mother bought a second set for him afterwards, for his football and things like that.) We used to row over who was going to watch the film and who was going to watch the match on Saturdays. As he got older we began to discuss things; this was from the time he was about sixteen. He went to De La Sallein Churchtown and we would talk about things that interested us both. There was no communication block even though we'd have major, crazy rows. I think these arose out of the mess I was in myself. He idolised Catherine. In the photographs we have he is always playing with her. She was like a baby sister to him, the only one he had.

We had got a postcard from him after he went away, saying that he had found work at a place called Béziers about fifty miles from Nice in the south of France, and that he was staying on there for a couple of weeks. Apparently he was with some guys from Galway and they went for a pint. He wasn't a heavy drinker, nor did he take drugs. He wanted to keep fit because he was soccer-mad. He said he was going back to the youth hostel because he had to be up early for work and that was the last they saw of him. It was a stormy night; there was a river. We don't know what happened. All kinds of things ran through our heads. We're very lucky to have got his body back but the mental agony during the time he was missing was intense. I can understand what people go through when a child or a relative disappears. For two weeks we knew he was missing and we knew it wasn't like him. If it had been me they'd have said, 'Oh she's gone off,' but my brother was very reliable and his passport and all his money were still in the hostel. We knew there was something seriously wrong.

All the way-out things that go through your head at such a time! Has he been kidnapped? Is he being abused? His body was so badly decomposed when they found him that they could only identify him by a tooth. He had been in the water for two weeks. He came back embalmed in a lead coffin. It meant that we didn't really know what had happened. He could have been robbed or even murdered for all we knew; there was no way of telling. It was a rough time and the hurt nearly killed my mother

It was a really bad year. I didn't do so much drugs (apart from the drugs I was given for medical reasons) but I drank a lot. It was alcohol, alcohol, alcohol all year. I just worked to drink. I was still at the Apollo and doing well, even after my operations. I had a huge scar on my stomach but I was still on the job, wearing glamorous make-up to cover the mark. It was crazy but I didn't care. I totally abused my body. My daughter is the only reason I'm alive. I wanted to die but I couldn't because I knew I had her and it would have been unfair.

We were terribly cut up about Damien's death but we had to live with it. It was a hard time and I don't know what got us through. Then Dave decided to go back to America. My mother had moved house again after my brother died, to the Navan Road. His school was right in front of her house and it was a constant reminder. I moved back home as well. I had fallen in love with a politician.

One of the problems I had at the time was the doctor with whom I had the arrangement to trade sexual services for morphine. When he visited me on a sick-call he'd phone me in advance to make sure my mother wasn't there. As soon as my daughter was old enough he'd give her money to go down to the shop for sweets. I was able to stay off the heroin because he was giving me all I needed of pure morphine. I had to break the connection with him as my doctor because the time came when I wanted to get away. He had been giving me morphine in a phial and he was skin-popping me with that and leaving me the needle he'd used and phials of morphine to use myself. When I wanted to give it up I said to him, 'Give me a bottle of physeptone [the same as methadone, a heroin substitute]. I want to stop it,' and he said no. He used to give me Temgesic tablets and I used to crush them and snort them. They are given to heart patients; there's an opiate in them called buphrenorphine. I'd take anything to get that hit. Drinking cough bottles with alcohol, anything just to get the buzz. All I was looking for was escape.

Eventually I cut him off myself. I just said, 'That's it,' and I changed my doctor. For an addict to cut off a line of morphine is hard, and I had a big line with any amount I wanted.

To get back to the politician. Dave had decided to go back to America so we broke up. I started seeing the politician and it was getting heavy as regards going away together and so on. Dave asked me to spend the last night with him. I wasn't going to because I was into my politician but I went. I saw Dave because I knew I might never see him again – which I haven't. We went for a couple of drinks and a meal. I told the politician I was staying in. I lied to him and it was one of the biggest mistakes I ever made. I should have told him the truth. The day Dave went to America I did tell him I'd been out with him and then the seriousness just went. He said to me, 'I can't trust you any more.'

From then on we just saw each other on a casual basis. It was stupid to lie but I knew that I was never going to see Dave again. Of course the politician knew where I worked and what I did. I knew (and so did he) that we could never be together permanently because he was in politics and I was involved in the business that I was in. It had been very serious but we could never have managed to stay together; his position and my profession meant that there could never have been a marriage or a settled future.

7

BLUEBELLS TO MANHATTAN

All these incidents helped me to make decisions. I wouldn't say I moped over things because I've always been the kind who says, 'Well that's it! It's gone! Get on with your life.' I strikes me now that I probably broke the trust between the politician and me deliberately for his sake because I knew we couldn't go on. That was another thing I realised: I was having to give up the people I loved because of the business I was in. I chose it and there are sacrifices I have had to make. For instance, losing my daughter is one of the prices I paid. I didn't choose a job instead of my daughter. I did not go into prostitution thinking, I'm going to lose my daughter. I didn't fully realise what it would entail.

The affair with the politician had cooled down and I had to do something about my physical health. The operations had had terrible consequences although they had saved my life. I had the menopause even though I was barely twenty-one years of age. The owner of the Apollo took me away on a holiday to Spain after one of my operations and I remembered the sweat pouring out of me. I remember trying to blow-dry my hair but having to give it up because of these sweats. The night sweats were even worse and there was also insomnia. I remember at the time listening to a radio programme in which all these older women in their fifties were talking about their lives and the menopause and a lot of them were naturally feeling sorry for themselves. It *is* a rough time. I tried to get through – unfortunately the lines were busy – to say, 'I'm twenty-two years of age and I'm going through the same thing. You've had your life.' In saying this I am not ignoring their feelings.

I left the Apollo and the Lycus because it got too heavy with drugs. I had a friend Lucy whom I met in the Apollo. She was strung out on heroin and died a while back. She and I worked Waterloo Road together later on. I remember exactly the time I left. I was sitting in the Lycus one Sunday on my own – on a Sunday you worked on your own – and this girl who also worked there, a drug addict, rang to make sure I was in. She asked me if I had done a customer – I had done five that morning – so she knew there was money there. The next thing I knew the door was coming in on top of me. I ran down and shut it so the intruders couldn't get in. They were drug addicts coming in with weapons to get the money. That was it as far as I was concerned. It was happening in every brothel in Dublin. We weren't being protected in any way.

I had a spell in a parlour in Belvedere Place. A taxi-man told me that I should go up there: 'They're flying up there,' he said and at first I thought was in business. I went to a place called Bluebells, a dump, but the owner had lovely girls and I became very popular there. I really got a good clientèle and made a lot of money. I got quite close to the owner and got to know her boyfriend. We always went out for a few drinks together after work. She was going away and she asked me to have sex with the boyfriend. We *did* have eyes for each other but nothing had happened because of her. Anyway we were in Rumours one night and she said, 'Would you look after him while I'm away?' It was only for a few days but we ended up spending them together and there was a real chemistry. But when the owner got back we didn't stop, and problems started.

Naturally she didn't want it to go on. I suppose she asked me in the first place because she knew he was going to be with someone and she preferred it to be me. She didn't trust him very far. He didn't have his own job so he was dependent on her. I had to have one last operation. Even though I was in hospital we kept seeing each other. It ended when he was killed in a car crash. We were still seeing each other and one night he was out with her and they were drinking. She was driving; he was killed and she was quite badly injured. A lorry ran into them on the Naas Road. She bounced back; she's still around. I've spoken to her since. It was very sad; I was in hospital when I heard about it.

It was in Bluebells that I met the conman I mentioned earlier. His personality just swept me off my feet. He was cheerful and seemed wealthy. It was the rule that you didn't see customers afterwards but he asked me to meet him and I agreed. Maybe I needed the money. I met him in the Royal Hibernian Hotel in Dawson Street. I spent a few hours with him that night and then left and went home to the Navan Road. That night I rang him when I got home. The following day he was going to America and I saw him for a couple of hours that day. When he got to America he rang me and every day we were communicating, a couple of times a day. Next thing he asked me to go out there. I flew to New York and he met me at the airport.

He was Irish, from Donegal, and he lived in Queens. He turned out to be a lunatic. I discovered that soon enough. We went to have a few drinks in Manhattan and my money disappeared from my wallet. I had a few thousand dollars in it. I suspected him immediately. I wasn't green any longer. The owners of the flat we were staying in said to me to get back to Ireland, that he was dangerous.

There I was, stuck in America with no money, so I had to go to work. I was in a pub (he was supposed to be working) and I said to this guy, 'In Ireland we have massage parlours. Where would I find them here?' He said, 'Over here you buy the local paper and look the places up.' I bought the *Village Voice*, and the first advertisement that appealed to me, I contacted the premises. They set up an interview and I arranged to go. I had to stay in the flat until I got some money together, and my Irish conman said, 'I'm going with you for the interview.' I said, 'I don't need you with me,' but he came anyway. He had a gun and all.

The interview went well but when I met the people on my own they said, 'We don't want him around.' I said, 'Fine.' It turned out that I was working for the Mafia. It was a fantastic agency to work in, I have to say. I was chauffeur-driven and had a magnificent wardrobe. My driver went everywhere with me; he would stand outside the door of wherever I was, or sit in the car outside the hotel. I was protected from the moment I came out, plus I got £500 an hour. The standard of customers was very high. It was there that I got the idea for vetting customers. The Mafia made big money out of it but I have to say they were gentlemen to work for. I know they were gangsters but they acted like gentlemen and I was protected. That's the part I liked.

I'm sure they vetted all their girls because everybody I met was excellent. They were so precise when I went for the interview: Do I do lesbian shows? Do I take drugs? I answered no to that question because over there you're talking heavy drugs. They were equally precise about the customers and their requirements. There was no messing around. This research did not go on in Ireland. It was then that I got my idea. I would set up a similar business in Ireland with the same kind of vetting and protection.

I felt very secure in America because all my minders were armed. Each protector would have a gun. The places I went to were amazing, beautiful; there was no sleaziness whatsoever. I was sent to some private apartments and to hotels and motels, all of which were secure and private. I never entertained anybody in my own place. The agency put me up in an apartment. The money I made over there, I really enjoyed; I saw Manhattan in a way you wouldn't unless you were a millionaire because all the money went on having good times. I had a fantastic time.

I met some fantastic people in the local pub in Queens. Some few were Irish but it was mainly American business-men I had dealings with. I can't say who, but over in America they'd be well known. They were customers but

I socialised with them.

I made several visits; the first time it was only supposed to be for two weeks but I ended up staying for a couple of months. When I came back the guy I had been over with followed me, even though I hadn't had any more contact with him. In America the people running the agency asked me did I want them to blow him away. I was still in touch with my politician here. He rang me at midday every day while I was in America, and when he found out who your man was he said, 'Get away from him.' That was when I ended up coming home and he followed me. I put him up because he was in hiding because of his past; he had been involved with the IRA. He even stole money from my daughter's money-box, that's how bad he was. Though I got rid of him eventually, he did stay with me for a while. In the end he got his marching orders.

The agency I worked for in America called me every week, every Friday night; they wanted me to go back. It was owned by a man and a woman and I found I was falling for him. That was no problem to her. They were just business partners. Every week he invited me back.

I was successful over there, I suppose. I think being so chatty helped and being Irish, maybe, but in America there's every nationality working in prostitution, like there is here now. Still I came back here again, immediately back into the situation I had left. I had no money. What else could I do? Where would I go? I had saved nothing; every penny I had went. I was living at a certain standard and never went below that. Besides, I couldn't stay away in the long term because of my daughter.

8

ON THE STREET

Dublin was nothing like what I'd just come from; it was
back to the seedy parlours again, to Mountjoy Square this
time, which was run by people I had met while I was
working in Bluebells. The place on Mountjoy Square was
a massage parlour, of course. They were all massage
parlours but there wasn't much massaging done. This one
was a death-trap; if it had gone on fire there was no safe
way out. It was rat-infested and the towels were all filthy.
But at least there were no drugs because even though I
was off the heroin I was still liable to be tempted. One
guy came straight out of jail to that parlour and offered
me a line of heroin. He left it in a Carroll's cigarette box
for me but I didn't take it. I think some other girl got it.
It was a case of swapping drugs for rats. The parlour was
really seedy. If a guy came to the door with £10 you'd be
expected to look after him for £5 and give £5 to the
owner.

It was not even very busy. The owner there had been
on the street herself and used to talk about it quite a lot.
The money was quite low because naturally the customers

were really penny-pinching. It struck me that if I was on the street the money would all be mine. In the place I was the presents I got were often stolen. There were klepto-maniacs there. I especially missed the gifts I got from a gorgeous friend of mine. She used to give me things for my birthday, or for any special occasion – porcelain and pretty things.

All this made me want to get away from the parlour. After my experiences in America I just couldn't stay with that sort of arrangement. It was then I got the courage to go on the street, although it was nerve-wracking at first. One of the girls who had been in the Apollo with me had done it. I knew Fitzwilliam Square was the place to go but I was terrified because I'd heard so many stories about the regulars not letting you work there. So I started working in Waterloo Road. At the time it had died as a working area but my friend and I brought it back to life. This was my friend Lucy from the Apollo days. One night I met her in a pub when I was trying to get out of Mountjoy Square. When I asked her where she was I discovered she was in Waterloo Road, and she asked me to join her there. I started there that very evening. I did three customers and was delighted with myself. It was all car work at the beginning but it was quick money. Within a couple of weeks the place was buzzing and we were flying. There were still only the two of us there. There were girls on Burlington Road but we never went near there. Sadly, Lucy later died from the effects of drugs.

I continued to work the road, the only girl there for some time. The Burlington girls were still there but I didn't bother them and they didn't bother me. I had built up my own list of regular customers. The idea behind my going on the street was to get money to get an apartment, a high-class apartment, so I worked the street every single night.

The family moved from the Navan Road to Kingston, a beautiful house near Ballinteer. I loved it, the wildlife, the lack of traffic, and I visited my daughter as often as I could.

It was very hard on me in the beginning because all the customers wanted a girl with her own flat, which I didn't have. I was working the cars, which was really dangerous. You could have a knife up to your throat. I would forego the money rather than take a risk. Generally I'd know customers going by but just the once when I'd had a few drinks – I never normally drank when I was working – that was when I got the knife to my throat. It was this guy I'd said no to many times before, but with the drink I didn't care and I got into his car. I don't know how I got out of it. I think he wanted to rob me but it was Ailesbury Road where so many embassies are, and I knew that there were guards along the road and that if I shouted I'd be heard. So I did shout. It's a wonder he didn't stab me and go. As it was, he left me in the middle of nowhere with no clothes. The guards didn't arrive and there was no point in involving them.

Another time a customer took me up the mountains and my life was in his hands. He could have killed me and just left me there and nobody would have known. I just picked him up on the road. I was wrong about him too but usually I could tell the ones to avoid. I'd been in the business for so long that there were many guys whom I recognised as messers from my time in the parlours. I just slammed the door in their faces. I would do without the money, say no, make excuses if I thought they were dodgy. I was always as careful as I could be.

When I was working on the street, I used to frequent a heavy inner city pub. The rough diamonds all went there but I used to go there every night, because some of them were fabulous people and I liked them. There were lunatics but I was a lunatic then myself. My best friend John would sit there with me. We'd always have a drink; then we'd go off clubbing or whatever.

I hadn't been involved with anyone for some time. After the politician I had a brief whirl with one of the younger sons of a Dublin family that was involved in crime but that didn't work out. I met him on New Year's Eve in the inner city pub I used to frequent; he just came up to me. I was with this other guy whom I took up with and who turned out to be a psychopath. I met all these guys as part of the gang in the pub. We'd sit together and everybody would know everybody else.

This psychopathic guy sold hash and I ended up moving with him into a flat in North Great George's Street. He was the next big love really, the first serious relationship after the politician. I stopped working for a while, then ended up going back on the streets. He didn't want me to work but we'd no money. I wanted to go back on the street. He brought me out and he spent money on clothes for me before I started. He'd drop me there and wait for me in the car. It was real pimpy – horrible. My earnings on the street were what we lived on.

The relationship started getting very nasty. He was on

the run from the guards, on their wanted list, and a lot of them knew his face so we couldn't go out together. He had to get out of North Great George's Street because the guards were getting to know that he was dealing drugs in the area. We moved to an apartment in Kimmage and that was when the trouble really started. I couldn't go outside the door. He never wanted me to be with anyone I knew and he was starting to become obsessed. We were constantly arguing and rowing. Though there was no physical violence at that stage he used to get into this no communication jag. This 'just keep your mouth shut' business used to drive me mad. Of course I wanted to be with my daughter, while he actually wanted me to go to England with him. I stayed off heroin while I was with him but I was drinking very heavily and I had also started to take Ecstasy.

The family had been very happily living in Kingston at this time. I claimed my unmarried mother's allowance but it all went to my mother since she looked after Catherine. I lived on the money I earned but I still paid bills and got things done to the house. When I met this man I moved out and my mother sold the house and went back over to the Navan Road again with my daughter, to a house near to her sister's.

Eventually we gave up the apartment in Kimmage and he got a flat in Inchicore. I was still working on the street and I used to be afraid he was following me, which he was sometimes. We hadn't seen each other for a couple of weeks when I happened to meet him, probably not by accident, now that I think of it. He asked me to come with him for a coffee down in the Waterfront and I agreed. I ended up going back to the flat with him and we had a great night. I said I was going home and went downstairs to ring for a taxi. I picked up the phone and then, all of a sudden, he jumped from the top to the bottom of the stairs, grabbed me by the shoulders and started head-butting me, viciously. I kept shouting, 'Stop, stop!' and the guy in the front room heard and came out. By the time the taxi arrived my head was swollen like a balloon.

After that the guy started stalking me. He used to lurk outside my mother's house. He was freaking me out, my daughter was freaking and so was my mum. I used to be afraid working on the street if I saw a car hanging around. I don't know what his appeal was. Initially it was that I was in love with him. I met him because he was a hash dealer and I was getting some stuff. He seemed quiet and different from the usual run. That was probably why I wanted to find out more about him. Some of the time we were together was really nice. We used to spend an awful lot of time in this gorgeous big double bed, a kingsize bed, eating and drinking wine and talking. But he turned out to be a true mystery man and the more I tried to find out about him, the less I discovered. Of all the men I've ever met he was the most mysterious. The stalking got so heavy that I think I did contact the guards about it. Eventually he fizzled out and went back to another girlfriend.

When I was working the street I worked early – in winter I'd be on the street at half six in the evening and I'd be gone by nine or ten. I didn't like to work after the pubs closed. I was really protective of myself on the street. I'd always make a couple of hundred pounds in that time but then some customers would delay me and I'd have regulars waiting for me. I didn't really spend long with each score. It was just ten or fifteen minutes at the longest.

The men were much more excited on the street. This was probably due to fear. Also they would be going around for hours until they got the girl they wanted, all the while getting more excited.

I worked on the street day in, day out and eventually I got an apartment in Clanwilliam Court. It was beautiful and the security was sky-high. We had a gate that was closed at night and there were loads of offices around so there were hundreds of people going in and out of the gate during the day. Even the guards used to come to me – and I used to charge. I was insistent; I'd say, 'No way! I'm not looking after you for nothing.' I met one of them later on at a major drugs raid on a rave, and we had a laugh together.

It took me two years to manage it. I had my own phone, not a mobile, but I had the phone in the apartment. It was a luxury apartment, it was safe and I could bring back the good customers. I'd still work from the street. It was great because I didn't have to go as far as Waterloo Road. I'd be just outside my door and there'd be customers pulling up. There were many nights when I didn't have to go out at all because every customer I met was OK. I'd give them my phone number and the phone was ringing all the time. If I met a guy and he wanted to spend the night I could charge up to £500.

On the street you were your own boss; that's what I liked about it. You could say no to a customer if you didn't like the look of him, whereas in a parlour you couldn't. I liked the freedom. Not that it wasn't low sometimes, especially in a car. That was the downside. Hand relief would only be £10, though sometimes you'd get £30. Most of the good customers were prepared to pay big money but they wouldn't go in a car. There were a lot of very well-known men, public figures, who used to pick up girls on the street at the time. They were usually too afraid to go in cars, although some did. It was crazy, the risks these really well-known guys would take: politicians, businessmen, professional men – guys from all walks of life. They would go in a car in the car-parks of Sandymount or way out to the ESB pillars in Ringsend. It was so dangerous because other girls would know these spots and they could be waiting in gangs with golf clubs ready to rob the customer and the girls. It got really dangerous. I knew then that I was on a mission on the streets but I needed at least £1,500 to £2,000 to get a luxury apartment. That was a lot of nights' work when you consider my living expenses and the standards I was used to.

When I was established in Clanwilliam Court life got better. Some nights I didn't have to go out. When I did have to go out, it could be frightening. I'd have a lot of girls threaten me. I remember a funny incident that happened when I was walking down Waterloo Road, my usual beat. As I said, I'd built up quite a list of regular customers, and one night I was very busy on the road and a couple of cars pulled in for me. When this happened I'd go first to the one I knew. I was walking by and one guy pulled in for me and I kept walking. Then this other car tried to pull in but the first one went into reverse and the two of them collided. I just kept walking on and avoided the two of them. I found that quite funny.

By now I was in my late twenties and on hormone treatment, and I was finding things very difficult, with insomnia, headaches and menopausal sweats. I had been on one hormone tablet a day since I was twenty and it is quite a chore to remember to take that tablet every single day. There were days you'd forget. Sometimes I'd have just taken it and the next minute I'd say to myself, 'Did I take it or not?' The requirement of having to take it every single day and knowing it was going through my liver was severe. If I didn't take it my body would go into turmoil, with sweats and insomnia. I was battling with the mess that had been made of my system. Even with the pill I was still getting hot flushes and my body was in an awful state, totally uncomfortable. When I went to have a review done I was put on a much stronger medication called Premarin. I'll be on a high dose of Premarin for the rest of my life; the higher the dosage the higher the risk of my developing cancer.

I kept on drinking. I always ate in the best restaurants and I had the best of wine and brandy. I wouldn't just have an ordinary brandy; I'd have to be on vintage champagne in Leeson Street till seven in the morning. I took the odd bit of cocaine but I always fell back on my security, the alcohol. I used to arrange that I would stop work as early as I could. I would always have a meal when I left the street. Even if I went home I'd have a naggin of something. I'd always have a drink.

I kept in touch with my mother and my child. I'd stay

with them as often as I could. I had the apartment in town but I didn't really stay there, except maybe the odd night when I partied late. I'd work there and make a few bob up to five o'clock and then come home early. I was still earning great money; my mother was getting extensions on her house, the garden done, a new car again, walls built, gorgeous furnishings, no lack of anything. By this time she was gradually giving up her own work. She still minded two children, which was great for my daughter. Catherine was now well advanced in school and had made friends.

If I wasn't in work I had no money. What I was doing was illegal so I couldn't pay tax or PRSI – the government wouldn't recognise me. But you could say I *did* pay my taxes because every penny went back into goods in this country, not a penny was put into accounts outside it, unfortunately. It went mainly on alcohol and cigarettes.

9

SETTING UP EXCLUSIVE ESCORTS

From the time I was in America it was in my head to get myself organised, to run things the way they were run there. There was still nothing like it here. When I came back here and saw the seediness, the lack of protection, the low pay, I was ashamed. We were part of the EEC at the time and were still completely unbusinesslike when it came to prostitution, while in every other country in Europe it was run strictly on business lines. There were no escort agencies in Dublin, just parlours. The best of them wasn't much better than the worst. Maybe one would have a nice décor but when it came down to the basics of money and protection there was no real difference. Anyone could knock on the door and get in. Most were run by men, although there were one or two, the one in Mountjoy Square and the one in Belevedere Place for instance, that had a woman boss. All of them were miserable sordid places, and against the law because it is illegal to operate a brothel. The idea was: just make as much money as you can and if the guards close you down in one place open up again that same week in another place. That is still being done.

It really is all a question of attitude. The people involved feel that the business is dirty. The men have pimpish instincts and they don't seem to see the sordidness of the way things are. There is the odd exception but the majority are like pimps. I suppose it's because they have never been on the game themselves. Even if the owner had been a customer (most were!) it's still not the same. If a girl is feeling upset and needs support a man can't give it to her but when you've been on the job yourself you know exactly what's required. I'd worked at it for fifteen years; I was a prostitute myself so I knew exactly what the girls needed and wanted and what the customers wanted and needed.

I thought to myself, if I do open an agency, who have I got to fear. And the answer was: the guards and the *Sunday World;* so I went to both. I told the guards I was opening an agency. I'd had it my mind for a long time but I didn't get it going until the beginning of the 1990s. I went to Kevin Street because I knew some of the guards there from previous dealings I had had with them. One of the detectives said, 'If you're ever opening your own situation, let me know about it.' So that's what I did. I just said it and nothing was asked or said. I also went to the *Sunday World.* I hadn't actually opened at this stage but I told them that I had an agency going and that it was being run as a high-class operation: £500 a night, £150 for the introduction. Nobody would get an appointment without a phone number or a credit card, and I would check them out in my own time. I had to know who I was dealing with and if the customer wasn't prepared to give

me those details and trust me, he wouldn't get an appointment. It took me years and years to build my trust up with
the customers but I eventually succeeded.

I started the agency in 1991, using the first article in
the *Sunday World* as a test. Because the response in the
paper was so good I decided I could afford to go on a
holiday. I was going to go to Tahiti to one of these little
straw huts with no electricity. I just wanted to get away
from it all. I was still working on the street at that time.
My doctor friend/customer said, 'I'm going away. Why
don't you let me take you?' So I trotted off to the Caribbean and while I was over there I noticed the huge
possibilities in providing companions for the very wealthy.
It was then I began seriously thinking that if the home
market proved sound I should consider an international
agency.

It was about this time that I decided to use the name
Marese officially. I used to have the name Lisa. I always
picked one that sounded like Louise because if I was out
and a customer called me and called me by my working
name, I'd be able to cover it. I was Marese when I was a
working girl and it was a lucky name for me because I
made a lot of money from it. When I decided to start up
the agency and I went to the papers my first interview
was with Dave Mullins of the *Sunday World* and he wanted
to know my name. I thought, oh God! I said, 'Marese' and
he said, 'Marese who? O'Shea?' I said, 'Yeah! O'Shea.' So
Marese O'Shea was born and it was the first time I really
felt I had a name of my own.

The agency started off as Exclusive Escorts because the
idea was that we would be totally exclusive. The girls had

to work exclusively for themselves. If they had any connection with other agencies it was dangerous for me and for the customers and for them. The idea, initially, was to ride all the publicity for two or three years and then to put in place a members-only policy, which it did come to eventually. My ambition was to have six to ten thousand customers worldwide and I got at least six thousand. They're are all filed in code now on a computer disk, every name and number. I'm the only one who has access. No one else would look at it; nobody would ever be able to break that code, although I can reactivate the system any time I feel like it.

My girls had their own apartments, so there was no question of a brothel. If a girl was on her own it was fine but once there were two women in a house it was classed by the law as a brothel. I never had a brothel in my life and wouldn't have anything to do with girls who were running brothels. Initially when the story went out in the *Sunday World* my phone number was given and of course girls and customers started ringing me. I had no business set up at all; all I had was an apartment. Of course all the publicity really got me going.

I did it like that deliberately to see what the reaction would be before I took a risk. I interviewed a few girls and met some stunningly beautiful women, intelligent, vibrant, full of life – career women. They were everything I was looking for and the sort I felt a man would want as well. A woman who had it all, who was independent – and I did find a few of those girls when I interviewed – was the sort of woman that I needed. These women wanted me to act as their agent and this was the way I wanted to work. I wasn't going to be their boss. They were my bosses; they employed me. None of them had their own apartments; they were all working on the street or in seedy parlours.

Initially my best girl, Amanda, worked in my apartment while I went out although she entertained mainly 'out', usually for full evenings. I didn't rush things; I took them very slow. When I met her she was on the street, earning very little money. She was a very hard worker, prepared to go anywhere at all hours. She was on her own. Her husband had left her with a child and she was educating this child, giving her a really good life, doing her best for her. He'd tried to take her child away to another country and she was caught in court battles for which she didn't have the money so she was working really hard to earn it. She was also putting money together to get her own place. I gave her most of the work she had and she was fantastic.

Of the £150 minimum per introduction, the girl got £100 and I got £50. If she got more on top of that, that was her own. As time went on, I would give all the girls who came to me house calls or hotel calls or country work until they got their own place. Or they would go to the customer's house as I used to do myself and it was quite nice. I had the customers vetted so the girls knew there were no messers involved. They knew it was straight and safe. I'd tell them exactly what I knew, like this guy is just back from wherever. There were so many different types of customers and some had been abroad. There was a guy who had just come back from Romania. He was a cameraman and his experiences had been horrific. His head was really messed up after what he saw and every day for a week afterwards he had to have someone to talk to. This was before the situation in Romania had really been publicised so the public here didn't understand about it, but all the girls I sent him supported him on that. The service involved a lot of different things; it wasn't just sex.

It developed from there, with Amanda, the original girl, initially in my apartment and others doing outside calls. I was out handling the business side of things, mainly by phone. Then I met a certain customer who had rented a townhouse with another guy, a business contact of his. He rang for a couple of girls. I went out on the job with another girl. We arrived at the luxury townhouse and found our customers, two businessmen. We had wine first of all before we went out for our meal, just to get to know each other. I couldn't help noticing that my customer was quite attractive. As the night went on I became more and more attracted to him. There hadn't been an awful lot of customers that I fancied but I found him and his way of going on rather fetching.

Twelve o'clock came and it was time to go. He went to get money on his credit card to pay us to stay on but there was no money there. He tried to give me some excuse but I knew he didn't have the money. I said that we were going unless he got the money. I don't know how he worked it but somehow he got the money and we stayed. We'd been out for something to eat and we'd been wined and dined. We had danced and come back. He dropped me in a taxi, saying he was getting out in town. He gave me all these lies but at the time I thought they were true. He said that he was separated from his wife, that he had his own business in town, which was quite well known, and of course he was staying in that posh house so I thought he was genuine.

Nights passed and he rang me. I was still in Clanwilliam Court and by now one or two girls had their own places. I was there myself running the phones. He came up to visit me and I still found him nice and attractive. He told me all about his children – he had five – and next thing, he moved in with me. It ended up that he started living with me, staying over most nights. Then out of the blue he gave me all this stuff that his business was in trouble, that somebody had ripped him off and someone else wouldn't pay him the money he was due. I was getting on to the contacts I knew to help him out; I really believed the guy.

From then on we were living together. He was doing only a couple of hours work a day, if that, and it turned out that it was all lies; he was still living with his wife and children, he had no business and he was penniless. Then one day I got a phone call from his mother at the apartment. I don't know how she got my number, though I could guess, and that night he arrived at my apartment with his five children, aged four, eight, ten, twelve and sixteen. His wife had thrown him out. So I took them in and pretended that everything was OK for the children's sake. It was them I was protecting. I couldn't bring myself to say, 'Go home,' because she wouldn't let them in. The children were all in a dreadful state; they all had fungal infections and one of them had a perforated eardrum. I brought him to the Eye and Ear Hospital. They were neglected and they were all a mess mentally.

At his stage my business was becoming really success-ful and a second story had come out in the *Sunday World*: gay guys were ringing me and asking me if I would act as their agent. I think everybody in the country was ringing me and asking me would I act as their agent. The pressure on me was immense, with the media, radio shows and these children still with me. The guy was separating from his wife at this time. He had told me so many lies that I didn't know what to believe. I don't know why I didn't just tell him to go. He was so manipulative and so persuasive that he roped me into a situation. I had to move from the apartment at Clanwilliam Court because of the children; there were no children allowed. That was when I moved to a marvellous apartment down on Merrion Road.

The apartment was in Merrion Court; it was huge and spectacular. There were three bathrooms with gorgeous tiles from all over the world and marble from Africa. The guy and the children were still with me. I agreed that *he* could stay until things were sorted out but that they would have to go. They needed their mother, especially the four-year-old. They went to court and got an agree-ment that they could see the mother. But she wasn't going to have them back and the children were devastated. And there I was, trying to keep them secure mentally, at least up to a point, especially the four-year-old, who started calling me Mammy. It was crazy. They were there about five or six months, morning, noon and night.

I was still trying to run my business; that was essential because I was supporting us all. They'd be in another room or I'd get him to take them out because I couldn't talk while they were there. It was all very wearing. My health was deteriorating rapidly because of the strain. I just couldn't cope with the five of them. It was heart-breaking. The man had effectively left his wife before he met me but he was still living in the same house as her and she didn't know he was off with other women. When they went to court the judge allowed them to see their mother at weekends but the four-year-old used to be ripped apart. You wouldn't believe the screams of her across the canal; the father would be on one side of the canal and the mother would be on the other and the little one wouldn't want to leave her mother. I constantly argued with him over it. The mother didn't want them; both father and mother were playing games with these children, ripping them apart, destroying them, using them as the ball; it was disgraceful. Of course I was the only one who was trying to mediate between the mother and the father with the children, in order not to turn them against either parent. They became really close to me.

I used to take on an occasional customer myself, just to escape, believe it or not, to get away from it all. That's when I started seeing the rock star. I saw him on a regular basis and I was living in his world. It was great and I didn't want to go back to my apartment, to the man or the five children. I started staying out and taking cocaine again. It was really quite bizarre when I think of it that the guy with the kids was living in my expensive apart-ment and I was hardly using it at all.

The rock star was a brilliant musician and great crack but he had a very lonely existence. Because of who he was he couldn't just go out and meet people. You'd think that stars like him would have all the women in the world at their feet but they don't. It's very hard for them to meet somebody. I was with him for a while and then I started going out with this other guy who had a club in Dublin, a nice jazz club. More and more I didn't bother coming home to the man with the five children. Because of all the hassles in my life I wasn't able to see my daughter as much as I wanted to, either, and I felt guilty about that.

Then your man started getting possessive: 'Why wasn't I coming home?' If I'm honest I had known nearly from the beginning that there was no future in the relationship. My main concern now was to get him out of my life but because of the children and the way things were, it was difficult. That guy used me to pay his debts as well. He just destroyed me, robbed me blind. I even bought his son a motorbike for his sixteenth birthday. All my money went. We had to get out of Merrion Court then. At this stage the court cases were going on about his separation and he used me to finance them too. I got him a great solicitor. His family squabbles were going on well before I met him; I wasn't the cause. In the end we moved out of Merrion Court with the children and went to a house on the Navan Road.

10

NATIONWIDE

It was then I started these nationwide tours. I had to travel around Ireland to find places for the girls to go to work, checking accommodation to see was it safe and private. I also made a point of having access for wheelchair users and handicapped people – something that had never before been considered in this business. Up to this the customer would have had to find a suitable place to take a girl. My experience of looking after disabled customers down through the years had made me very aware of this. During the time of the nationwide tours there were days when I had ten girls going to ten different places: Cork, Limerick, Clare, Clonmel, Waterford, Athlone, Monaghan, Galway, Sligo, Donegal, Drogheda and Dundalk were being covered. International calls were coming in. The *Sunday World* headline was: 'Goodtime Girls Go Nationwide.' The story included my telephone number.

This would be the public introductory line. If the customers didn't reach me, they would be given an alternative number where they would hear a recording I had made of the weekly touring timetable. Then they could leave their number or call me back. Monday was Limerick and the northwest; Tuesday the North and the southwest; Wednesday was Waterford and the midlands; and so on. Some days I'd have seven different centres covered, plus Dublin (twenty-four hours a day, seven days a week) and Europe. Tough work, and the service was available all the time.

Initially I didn't cover the North but then I said why not. If customers rang me from the North I would put them on file and get in touch with them when someone was going up from Dublin. I also had girls on my books who were based in the North but who would cover the northwest and the border areas and would also occasionally join the rest of the goodtime girls on their tours. Every Tuesday we would cover Belfast. Once I got in touch with people who made private houses or apartments available to us, we used this accommodation rather than hotels.

Nobody had ever gone to the country and there were a lot of men down there who needed company just like people in Dublin – a lot of farmers especially, who couldn't leave their land or their animals to come to Dublin. There was no danger of anyone finding out. The accommodation would be way out in the sticks, quite luxurious. I'd rent a nice house in the country or a private townhouse and the girl would go there, with a driver of course. I'd never send a girl on her own. (Hotels didn't really work unless you had only one customer and it was very difficult to guarantee privacy if he was known in the area. A lot of the customers were bachelors, wealthy farmers, who needed things to be discreet.)

Other agencies have since copied the system of using bodyguard-drivers. Before I set the trend, they used to send girls all by themselves into these crazy places in the middle of nowhere – no protection again! The girls could be killed; they could be lying there and nobody would know. They didn't even have mobiles. Whereas my girls had a driver; they'd pay or I'd pay a guy so much to drive them there. The driver would stay overnight with them and be their chauffeur, their protector. They'd light the fire for them and get the place warm. It was really cosy and the girls loved it. Going away to see a customer was the nicest trick of all. Girls would ring up and say, 'Can I go away and where can I go?' I'd know the customers in advance and I'd know who'd suit whom.

I did all the administrative work myself, with no secretary or word processor. I kept all my own records, handwritten but coded. Every single thing was coded, and every customer's name. I knew every customer from the phone. As soon as somebody said hello to me I knew by the way they said it whether I liked them or not. I could tell what they were like the minute they spoke, by the way they made their approach. There were lots of customers I just rejected. I'd starve before I'd give them an appointment because I knew they were abusive.

I once worked down the country myself and I liked it. It was the time of the separation battle involving the guy with the five children, and it was great to be away from it. All the girls said that the country customers were kinder, more genuine. I'd say they were easier to look after because some of the men in the cities quite regularly pay women for their company and therefore can be that bit more demanding. They want more; they expect more.

On one occasion, when I was checking out accommodation in the northwest, a guard, a regular customer, phoned me to ask if there was any girl in the area who would call in to see him. I said I was in the area and that I would come, although normally I didn't take customers myself any longer. He said he wanted me to come to the garda station and gave me directions to an old rural station in the west of Ireland. It was a very cold and wet night. My host had lit a lovely open fire and had a bottle of Hennessy open. One of the cells in the station had a bed and a VCR and he had brought in a blue movie. He was the only one in the station but the phone would ring now and again and I was terrified that we would be interrupted. I looked after him in the cell. He was in uniform and didn't appear to be nervous at all but I was a nervous wreck.

I found that as the years went by customers in general definitely expected more. When I started in the parlours, it was as if they were glad just to get in to meet some other woman, but as time went on they demanded a better standard of company. They didn't want a housewife who was stuck for money, who just went into the parlours and didn't look after herself. They wanted a woman who looked fantastic from head to toe, somebody who was out there doing whatever she wanted to do, someone with a life. The girls who had an air of being successful were very popular.

One thing about the girls: they were attracted to the job for other reasons as well as money. Of course the money was good but it was not just that. It was also the

good feeling you had when you were popular and guys
would come in asking for you. Well for me at least it was
great to hear someone ask, 'Is Marese on?' It was the sense
of being admired and constantly complimented that I
liked. I had the sense too of being different. As a child I
was always different; being adopted I felt unusual so it
was a familiar feeling. I'd block out the sex part. The thing
is, you don't have to have sex and I always knew I didn't
have to have it. If I ever felt I did, I got out of it quick.
Anyone I ever introduced to any of my girls was told that
sex was not guaranteed. I used to say this myself to every
customer: the £150 will cover the company, no more. I
would never put anybody, male or female, into a situation
where they had to do anything offensive. In case they
didn't even like the customer I'd say, ring me within the
first five or ten minutes and I'll get someone else. But I
was always right in my choice of who'd suit whom. It's
what I became known for.

My sense of who suited whom didn't always work in
my personal life. I was conned several times – by the guy
from Donegal with whom I went to America and the guy
with the children. I couldn't help my feelings, just
ordinary human feelings getting in the way. It was my
weakness and they exploited it. I suppose this happened
to me a lot as a child as well. At some level I knew by
now that I had lost my own child. While the family was
living on the Navan Road my daughter was around twelve
or thirteen. I think that was when I finally lost her. She
started smoking cigarettes and I knew somehow; my heart
was torn in two. My mother was constantly turning her
against me. She would say things like: 'She doesn't want you.

Look at her, living with another man and his children . . .' It was absolute nonsense, of course. It wasn't that way at all. She knew I had a dating agency, which it basically was, and she knew I travelled a lot, but I didn't see her half as much as I should have. At this stage my mother had moved house again, further on up the Navan Road.

After we left Merrion Road and before I got the house on the Navan Road I was in an apartment at the back of the Halfway House, Ashbrook. Things were very bad between your man with the five children and myself; he was constantly lying and I knew it. We were in town one day with my daughter and he suddenly went missing. I saw him cross the Ha'penny Bridge while my daughter and I stayed on the other side. We got a taxi on up to the house. Hours later he arrived and said he had walked all the way home. It was a freezing night. Yet he was warm as he came in the door and I knew he was lying. He used prostitutes, of course. As I said, I think it is an addiction and I believe he was seeing women even when he was with me. He just didn't have the guts to tell me.

It all ended quite cruelly. I became very vicious with him. We were constantly arguing and he wouldn't listen to me. The lies continued and I had proof of them. Eventually it came to physical violence and my health suffered.

Meanwhile the business continued to flourish. The girls were paid by credit card or cash. They would come back from the country with a lot of money. A few times one or two would go off without giving me my share but they always came back because they knew they wouldn't get another job until they paid me the money they owed me.

I could be on the phone from ten in the morning till two or four the following morning. They thought they could just do the work and take all the cash, forgetting about me toiling all those hours to get them work in the first place! I had a good few people out and about. Most of them admitted that there was nobody like me in this country or anywhere else probably. They knew that I was the best so they always came back and said, 'I'm sorry; will you let me work and I'll pay you the money I owe you?' I'd always forgive and forget.

It meant that there was no need for me to handle customers myself. I wouldn't have had five minutes free anyway. Money was coming in but I don't know where it went. I was living in an expensive place, travelling around the country and staying in top hotels, Waterford Castle and places like that. I had a lovely car and chauffeur most of the time, and my guy with the five children was creaming off his share as well.

I suppose I should have had a business partner, maybe even a man. I would try for one if I were ever to go back to the escort business full-time. I am conscious to this day that it is still dangerous out there for girls. There was a murder just recently, for instance. I tried getting someone to help me with the phone-answering but it didn't work. The customers would say, 'I'll wait until Marese comes back.' Names were never used, always numbers. Membership was by invitation; they couldn't just join themselves. A guy would ring me up and give his real name, credit card number and certain other details and then I'd allocate a number to him *if* I accepted him for membership. The system protected everyone, girls and customers alike – and me, of course!

The girls were under contract that they couldn't discuss anything about who they had been with after the meeting. I was very careful about the girls I acted for, so the customers were guaranteed discretion. It worked. There was not a single case of beans being spilled. A stage was reached when I had seventy-five or eighty girls in Ireland and I knew every one of them was one hundred per cent. The girls would let me know what hours they were available. They used to ring me and say, 'I'm on for such a time.' In turn I'd ring certain customers and let them know that a particular girl was available and when. If I had no girls on I would just turn the phone off or I'd say nobody was available, rather than taking a chance on somebody I couldn't trust. My business was all about trust.

11
——

GOING INTERNATIONAL

When I went on the Caribbean holiday with my doctor
friend I had a great time. I worked, of course, but not as
an escort. I found quite a lot of men, very wealthy men,
coming on to me. I noticed that there were many single
millionaires about and that the Caribbean needed my kind
of service very badly. I spoke to a few guys over there
and one day we went out to this little island. It's one of
those places that are quite deserted; you just go there for
lunch. It was very beautiful. I got talking to these interesting gentlemen and I was asked to provide my service over
there. I had reluctantly to refuse.

I did work in Spain, though. Any time I went on a
holiday I'd end up working in the country and I'd stay
longer. When I became internationally known a lot of
people used to make a point of seeking me out. Before I
became known I'd find the places to work, just as a
working girl myself. In Spain there are apartments and
you appear on the balcony. The guys can see you on the
balcony and come up and pick you. It's quite nice –
different. Wherever I went throughout the whole of

Europe I ended up talking on radio shows. Once I was on holiday on the French Riviera and when the local radio station heard about it I was asked to take part in a programme. It was the same when I was in Italy. I had become so well known because of the escort agency. I formed the plan then to set up over there on the French and Italian Rivieras.

My face was becoming known too. Those in the business, the customers, would recognise me because they'd have an interest in what I did. It's part of their life. On holiday these people would approach me saying, 'Can you arrange something for me?' That's what gave me the idea of going into Europe. The customers were Irishmen who were abroad. Irishmen out of their own country can be vulnerable. It can be very dangerous for them to use prostitutes so I started working on getting international contacts so that they would have security. I rang around. I knew agencies all over Europe because I'd checked them out in the countries I'd been in.

When I set up the international network I was simply extending the service that I gave at home. Particular girls who were on my books would say to me, 'I'm going abroad next week. Can you arrange someone for me over there?' So I would contact the best agency in whatever country it was. Usually I knew which ones were the best and if I didn't I would check each one until I found what I considered to be the best. I would have a customer or a colleague of mine check them out and come back to me. If I thought they were all right I would contact the owners and we would set up an exchange system. If they had people coming over here I'd make arrangements with them and if there were Irishmen going there, they'd be looked after by the best. Others might be going away with a customer, or a lot of customers, especially on these golf holidays, the ones organised by a club. The girls would be so good that when they'd meet the customers, the men wouldn't even know that they were callgirls, they fitted in so perfectly. That's how good they had to be to work for me.

Eventually I began to get invitations from people in some countries who asked me if I'd be interested in going over and running agencies there. An American agency asked me but I was too busy here. It was a New York agency and I'm sure it was Mafia-run.

I have to admit that foreigners are a bit harder to please than Irishmen; they're a bit more demanding and also more selective. I think this is because they use women regularly, especially men who travel the world. (I remember one customer said to me, 'I got your number in Japan.' He probably had it from some business connection.) When men have been all over the place they've had their pick of girls. They've probably met the kind of girl they want – Filipina, for example – and formed a particular taste. Then if a girl from a particular country is not exactly to their taste, they tell you. I wish more Irishmen would do that.

But even Irishmen are getting to be more demanding and that's one of the reasons I opened the agency. Then again, this country wants business and if you're going to be bringing in business then you've got to provide company as part of an evening's entertainment. Visiting businessmen are not necessarily married and there's nothing wrong with wanting the opposite sex; it's quite natural.

People from different countries have different sexual tastes. They also have different physical characteristics. In the Far East both men and women are much smaller in build and it does make a difference. There are also different cultural attitudes. The members of my agency know that they may have to make adjustments. I had to be ready to do this myself when I was working. But you don't have to be whisked off to Japan to meet those people because Ireland is full of different nationalities, especially from the Far East. There are a lot of Chinese people here and they are great tippers. They come along in gangs, ten of them at a time, and they all say they want the one person.

The oddest variation to Irish minds is fetishism. In America I found the most demanding of fetishists. A lot of people like to act out fantasies but in America they can literally have what they want: over there money buys anything. When you are working as an escort you're asked what you are prepared to do: lesbian shows, two guys – whatever it may be. But fetishes also include the backside fetish, breast fetish, face, neck, whatever. A true professional can work her way around anything; and in the end, if you don't like doing something you don't have to do it.

I remember a customer I had when I was on the street who had a fetish for stealing knickers. During the day he must have spent all hime time driving around Dublin 4, looking in gardens and checking which ones were easy to get into. He was on the street at least three nights a week. He would employ me for up to three hours just to accompany him as he drove around the streets and wait while he'd sneak into a garden he had already cased to steal knickers. He might steal up to five knickers in an evening. I'd have to wait for him in the car, terrified of being caught by a guard or the owner. After that he'd wear one of the purloined knickers to have a sexual climax. I think it gave him an added buzz if he caught a glimpse of the owner of the knickers in the vicinity – he'd climax immediately. I found the whole thing very harmless even though the customer never left the cost of the knickers on the clothes peg!

Speaking of knickers, I've sold many a pair. When I worked in the parlours, customers would call to the door begging the girls to sell their used underwear. They wouldn't come into the parlour – these men would be different from the regulars. Some of them would offer as much as £50; of course the cheapskates would try to get away with £5, even for an expensive piece of lingerie, and you would sometimes agree just to get rid of them. There was also demand for urine, which you could sell for £5 to £10 a bottle – although nowadays I wouldn't settle for less than £5,000 for a urine sample. A 'golden shower', where the customer would sit or lie down and the girl would shower them with her urine was quite a regular request, and the girl would get a good tip for this service.

It's much more enjoyable for the customer when he gets a companion who knows what is expected of her and is willing. It's a lot better than sending out a girl who is reluctant and unskilful; you're sending out someone who enjoys doing the work. I personally was never really into fetishism. Nor did I like hurting people. With the people who want that kind of thing, mainly domination customers, you don't have to touch them by hand at all. They are sexually fulfilled just by being whipped; the whipping excites them enough in their heads for them to climax.

Domination customers are not generally dangerous people. The real domination customer just wants to be beaten. One heavy domination customer from Cork came to me with his own whips. They were the height of the ceiling. You had to move the bed to get a good lash at him and he wanted to be beaten until he bled. That upset me so much I didn't do it any more. It is not my business or any other girl's to counsel these people who are essentially into self-abuse. Most people would say, 'Whatever turns them on . . . ' However, I have spoken to domination customers and with the majority it stems from boarding-school and what was done to them there. Their sexual fulfilment is wrapped up with what happened to them when they were abused. Maybe it eases their hurt. Without a doubt, the original abuser got his kicks from inflicting the pain. I just don't understand it. I couldn't hurt anybody. I think that with 'pain' customers, especially those into domination, their own domestic sex lives must have ceased. These guys go home with marks on them that take time to heal. You have to assume their wives don't get close enough to notice.

I do believe that some of these people need help but it's up to them to get counselling. Even when I was working myself I would spend hours talking to customers about their relationships. I felt they needed it and that it was a part of the service I was giving. I've really gone into depth in analysing it. Now I believe that with the proper counselling these sexual games can be transformed or even transferred to the customer's own partner – with her agreement, of course. A lot of men are afraid to tell their wives and partners what they would like in case they lose them. That's why they say they want to keep on going to prostitutes. For some of them it is a major problem. A once-off is OK but someone for whom it is a regular, say weekly thing, would need counselling. Their sexual preference becomes an addiction, like drink. Every penny of their money goes on prostitutes. It's what they live for: when they're not actually with a prostitute they're thinking of it, either what they did last time or what they're going to do next time. It's a preoccupation, an obsession even.

Fantasy customers are not easy; sometimes I used to come out with my head wrecked, especially after something really heavy. A couple of times guys had me acting as their sister or something. That would set off my own childhood memories and hang-ups. I could not handle that; even as sexual fantasy it scared me. Where's the line between reality and fantasy? I was always uneasy about what I would have to face from my own past. Someone getting very rough with me took it out of me as well. There were times when I'd come out and just cry. I would be so drained it would take me hours or even days to unwind. The more I got involved with people and the more they started talking about their problems the greater the effect it had on me. Every single day men would come in and pour out their problems. It really would upset me. In the end of it all, sex is a very small part of the whole business of prostitution.

I began to employ girls from Malaysia who had been

given visas by their own government. These were girls from a very deprived background and the initial arrangement was that they were to be employed in my apartment. This meant that I could be accused of exploiting these women. Alice Glenn rang up Pat Kenny's radio show to suggest that I was exploiting them and he asked me to go on and talk about it. I made it clear that I wouldn't exploit anybody. This may sound like a contradiction but in fact any work I did was to *prevent* girls being exploited.

Eventually the girls wanted to work for themselves. That was their reason for coming over; it wasn't as if I had to look for them. It hurt me that people should think that I was exploiting them so I knocked the whole scheme on the head. It wasn't worth it. The idea was exaggerated out of all proportion by the press. There were about seven girls in all and I looked after them well. I made sure that they were in good health and that they could look after themselves.

On the question of STDs (sexually transmitted diseases) I always knew that it was essential for prostitutes to make sure they were healthy, because sex is their business. I'm talking now about professional prostitutes, those who have chosen it as a career. Of course any of the girls who worked for me were absolutely safe. If I thought for one moment that any of them would perform unprotected sex I would not keep her. If I thought that my girls were taking risks, sleeping around, not necessarily with customers, I would still consider them dangerous and I wouldn't have anything to do with them.

All the customers had to accept that condoms were going to be used. Girls often came back and reported that particular customers were hassling them, not wanting to use protection. If a customer ever behaved like that again his membership was cancelled. Some of them would offer phenomenal amounts for unprotected sex – they even offered them to me – and these were people whom you would think highly intelligent! None of my girls was allowed to give unprotected sex, no matter how much extra was offered. Of course they were human and I would not be surprised if one or two were unwise enough to take the risk.

There was one girl who worked for me who was excellent. She loved dating and going out and enjoying herself. She got involved with a very successful Irish businessman and he started seeing her at home without my knowing. She took a risk and had unprotected sex. She came to me terrified but she had to suffer the consequences, I couldn't give her any more work or give the customer any more girls either.

When I started working, Aids was not a problem but venereal diseases were. The truly professional prostitute knows how to deal with these things. The unprofessional prostitute might not know that unless it's lubricated, a condom may burst. Yet I've seen prostitutes using oil on a condom, which makes the whole thing just rip apart. A professional would know that you should use KY Jelly and plenty of it. This doesn't apply just to prostitutes but to everybody who regularly use condoms, in or out of marriage. Even before Aids came I knew using a condom was vital.

My hysterectomy made things simpler for me. Whatever happened I wasn't going to become pregnant. Most working girls do run that risk and that is why relatively few are willing to give full penetration. Some women who work never ever allow full sex. I know a couple of lesbians who are prostitutes but they do not necessarily work with lesbian customers. They rarely have sex with their customers. They will perform all manner and kind of sexual acts but they won't actually have full sex.

When I was still working as a prostitute myself I knew a girl who had a child but she didn't know who the father was. She didn't even know if it was a customer's child. She had to pretend to her husband that it was his. The number of abortions that take place is very sad. Then again it's about ignoring precautions. Lack of education plays its part as well. A lot of girls would initially lie about their work to their husbands and partners. I could never understand that. I'm too open, I suppose, and that can be dangerous in other ways because I have paid for that honesty. If I met a guy and I knew I liked him I'd have to tell him the truth on the second date; I couldn't deceive him. The men soon see through the lie because they can't be blind to the fact that these women have so much money! But most men soon accept the situation; they are glad to be able to make use of their partner's money for their clothes and holidays and necessities.

The other girls – my friends when I worked the street – who were aware of my gynaecological condition used to say that I was so lucky not to have to worry. If only they knew ... There was one advantage: I didn't get monthly periods so I didn't have to use a sponge as the others did. I never had any STD in my life. Once I had a skin thing but it was from somebody in my own personal life. When I was working I'd use a special lotion on my skin. You leave it on for twenty-four hours and then you wash it off but the protection stays on your skin so you are less likely to get any infection. As I used to say always to my girls: 'Educate your customers!'

Professionalism is important in this business, maybe even more so than in many other fields. A service is required and should be paid for. There has to be at least an unofficial contract, with the rights of both parties taken into account. Most of the girls I knew (myself included) did it as a job for the cash it brought in. I did, however, have a very good friend, a beautiful woman with long blonde hair, who didn't need the cash. She had children she loved, two cars, a house in Stillorgan, everything that money could buy. Yet she'd ring me and say, 'Have you any work?' and afterwards: 'Marese, he was gorgeous!' She just loved the customers. She was wonderful and very popular. Her husband had no idea, although she used to bring customers home to her own house when he was away. The customers knew this because I had to let them know, but they were determined to see her. Because she was married she was unavailable quite often. So when her husband was away she'd phone me and I'd ring her favourite customers, who were so dedicated that they'd drive six hours to come up to see her for an hour even. On a few occasions they were close to being found out but the customers liked that, the buzz of it. I know in my own heart and soul that I couldn't deceive like that. I would make sure that the children of the man who was living with me wouldn't be in the house if I was doing any work myself. If any of the girls had children the kids would have to be out.

The secret of being a good escort is having the capacity to enjoy yourself at all entertainments. It is a very difficult and exacting job. When I was doing escort work myself I used to come home mentally drained. Just one customer and he would wear you out. You have to cater for someone else's needs in every way. That's why you need to be very strong to live as a prostitute. You've got to be an entertainer, yet live with the hurt of it. There's your own hurt and of course everybody outside is constantly hurting you as well, laughing and whispering. The social non-acceptance, the price you pay – no money would compensate you for it.

Everyone is in prostitution because of her social circumstances at the time. The prime motivation may not always be money – your own needs play a part – but it's an issue. It's not easy repeatedly to be intimate with a man for money and walk away from it unscarred. Very few people take the trouble to understand and you're just put down all the time.

The kindest person I know is a prostitute. Her name is Marion and she has a heart of gold. She gives so much of herself constantly and it's so rarely she gets it back. When my mother died I had no money. I was just out of Coolmine and I wasn't going back to prostitution. I was at a turning point. Marion took me abroad on a holiday and looked after me like a sister. Things had got so bad that I lost my home and was put out on the street. I had nowhere to go. She offered me a place – she was the only one to do so.

In general there can be a lot of bitterness and anger among working girls. The majority of them come from deprived and dysfunctional families. They feel let down and sore and usually don't have time for anybody else. They don't know any better. When I worked in parlours they treated me very badly too. A lot of them stole things from me and I had a very hard time. Many of them were suspicious of me and kept putting me down because I had a better accent than them and was educated. That accent caused me more than enough problems. It was so difficult for me to fit in. If I had had a working-class Dublin accent I would have been accepted immediately but I was always laughed at. Then I was popular and successful and that was another reason for them to hate me. Some of the girls who had treated me so badly had the gall to come and ask me for a job and I, like a fool, gave them a chance.

Yet I must insist that it was only a small minority of the girls I employed who ever tried to cheat me. Some went out and opened their own places without letting me know. There was no 'Marese, I'm going off to do my own thing.' They did the dirt on me and tried to steal my customers but it didn't work at all. My customers would be on the phone the same day saying, 'Marese, do you know what's going on?' I know it's normal business practice to set up on your own and take customers with you. I don't deny them the right and I wouldn't have begrudged it. But they lied to me and there was a deadly loss of trust.

12

PARTIES, STAG NIGHTS AND OTHER DIVERSIONS

All this talk of drugs and street work makes me realise how much better things were when I had the agency. I was happier, richer – and safer! – and so were the girls and customers. It was, as its name indicated, meant to be exclusive, expensive even. The very first thing was to get across to the customer what the rate was. A night was from eight in the evening to late – the early hours of the following morning – and the fee would be at least five hundred pounds plus an agency fee of one hundred and fifty. The girl got the hundred and I got my fifty. That fee was simply for the introduction but it brought with it the guarantee of quality, confidentiality and security. The other expenditure was agreed between the escort and the customer. An overnight, that is from the previous evening until the start of another working day, cost more than the basic five hundred but these terms were arranged between the parties. I got none of that money, although when making the introduction I laid it on the line what the costs were likely to be. Arrangements were made through me and if a guy rang and wanted to book someone for a full night, if he wanted to go clubbing afterwards, I'd say, 'There will be a minimum charge of six hundred and fifty pounds for that.' He might ask, 'Will she stay till morning?' and I'd say, 'You'll have to discuss that with the girl.'

If initial or subsequent arrangements didn't go through me, the customers didn't have the security, the privacy or the protection that the agency supplied. It was the same for the girls. They knew they could see the customers behind my back but if they did they were taking a risk. Most of them realised this and eventually, even though they might go off, they always came back to me. For one thing, they made more through me than they did on their own and they didn't have the hassle.

The fees were high in 1991 and even today they appear steep. Yet some guys would use my services for a week at a time. Big companies used the agency and paid by credit card but a lot of the money came out of personal pockets. To an ordinary person five hundred pounds is a lot but it's not that much for a very successful business-man. When we began to get foreign customers they did not find the rates excessive. Their numbers increased after I decided to advertise in the *International Herald Tribune*. Mine was the first Irish company ever to go on that network. I knew the *Tribune* from the time I worked in America and was aware that all the top agencies in the world advertise in it. As soon as I started using it I had a big influx of foreigners. I had known for some time what was the going rate on the continent and I wanted us to be on a par with the other European countries.

The girls soon learned that being in the agency was

much more profitable than being on their own. When I was on the streets that same year I started the agency, if you got a hundred from a customer you'd think it was fantastic. Exclusive girls would just do one customer and they'd have money to keep them going for a week. Then they might disappear for a time because they'd be earning so much money that they only had to go out once or twice. I didn't mind this disappearance because all my girls were excellent, hand-picked. When the agency was up and running I had between seventy-five and a hundred active escorts in the context of the thousand or so street prostitutes the city had at that time.

My own personal standards have always been very high. I have been through hell over the last year and I now have to start going to beauty salons again and looking after my skin and my hands. I always had soft white skin. It was my bank account and it made me a lot of money until I began injecting the money back in. I always had the best of underwear, clothes and perfume – everything. I was eating the top food, drinking the best wine. A bag of chips was a rarity; it was oysters or nothing. If it hadn't been for the drugs I would have had a very luxurious lifestyle. The girls, however, were all clean. None of them was an addict because my rules didn't allow it. I couldn't trust a drug addict, you see; they could rob a customer and there was always the risk of infection.

The business began to evaporate because my own habit got out of hand but that was near the end. A lot of the customers did cocaine, I'll admit. I was once asked on a radio show about this: was I not jeopardising girls sending them out to these wealthy men who did drugs? My answer was that the girls were all adults. The customer didn't say, 'Oh, by the way, Marese, I want a girl to do drugs with me.' It was up to the individual. Some girls didn't even tell me, although it should have been reported back. Others said, 'No way will I go with him again!' Nowadays the drug scene has got very heavy. The first time I left the street there wasn't anything like the amount of hard drugs that's about now. There's a lot of young girls, no more than sixteen, strung out, but usually they're run off the street by the other girls.

It was about this time that I thought about the idea of a contract. I needed it to protect the business. I knew all the girls and I knew their real names. They had to use their real names or the contracts were not valid. They were prepared to put that trust in me. Their business names were different of course. I had to cover the customers, too, as regards secrecy and discretion. Most of the customers were established businessmen who had a lot to lose. I had to try to find a way to protect them. I knew girls I couldn't trust even if they signed and I knew girls I could trust. I was in the business fifteen years and it's something I learned. The contract was like a guarantee: if plan A fails, it's plan B. All the girls signed it. I did have contracts with the customers initially but then there was no need for that. There were also a couple of girls who were top models and they asked for contracts and I had to give them one. They made more money with me than they did on the catwalk. One was an Irish girl; she was gorgeous and very popular. I think she had worked in prostitution and then broken into modelling. I was terrified the newspapers would get her so we had to keep it very low key.

Agency girls could be sure of a good career until they were about thirty-five on average, although there *are* men who will insist on older women. Younger men want girls of eighteen to twenty but older men prefer an older escort, forty, maybe fifty. I will never forget one of the most beautiful women I ever interviewed in my life. She was about fifty-five or sixty. She was bored, wealthy, well-educated and wanted male company. She wanted to work as an escort. Her skin was beautiful, her hair, her clothes, her jewellery, her style, her class were all superb. I can't reveal where she lived but she owned a floor of a beautiful Georgian house and her taste was spectacular.

She took customers back to her own place from time to time but it was never the norm for reasons of security. I'd say to the girls, 'It's not good to bring the customers back.' I advised them that it was better that a majority of customers should not know where they lived. It was better to go out, to an hotel or wherever. In fact we used to spread out a lot.

Of course in other hands the whole escort business became crude and dangerous again. As soon as I had set up the nationwide tours successfully, the next thing I realised was that all the brothels were doing it. They went down in droves to major provincial towns and cities. They were going in and destroying the business. Instead of a girl meeting one guy, she'd meet ten in a day. Eventually they were getting thrown out of the accommodation. I was the pioneer. I saw the chance, covered the ground when it was good, and then they all followed me down. I listened to people and I've always been aware what services are needed, not just this. This had all been in my head for years before I got the agency together.

It inevitably happened that some of the girls got friendly with their customers. I lost one girl when she got married to a customer, which was great for her. That gave me the idea of the Marese O'Shea Bureau, when I introduced people for long-term relationships and many ended up getting married. It was great. I'd introduce the gentleman to three people and out of that three I would have success on one. The charge for a successful arrangement leading to a long-term commitment was £1,500. The first payment was the usual £150 introduction fee. If the two people felt they wanted to stay together the gentleman would pay the balance.

There was a story at the time in the *Sunday World* with the headline 'Selling Irish Brides'. It was a bit sensational. I simply found suitable partners for people abroad. America was a huge potential market but I deliberately didn't get involved with America because there was so much on my plate at that time. But I could have concentrated solely on America, introducing American men to Irish brides. I never needed to advertise. My agency got known through word of mouth in America but I had to stop it because I couldn't even cope with the demand of Irishmen, mainly rural, looking for wives.

There was a distinction, of course, between the girls I matched with customers for temporary entertainment and those who purely wanted to meet someone and get married. That part of the business was really a marriage bureau. Those girls came to me as a result of another newspaper article. When it became clear that a lot of men and women were ringing me looking for a long-term relationship, I set up a totally separate phone line and list for that and it became huge immediately. I had to say to myself: 'Hold on here.' It was all getting too much for me. I suppose I have this knack for fitting people together. That's my thing, that's why I am who I am. Even recently when I went back and opened another agency under a completely false name it happened again. I did all the talking, explaining the way things worked, and immediately it took off. People started ringing back looking for me. It's an art, a talent, a way I have with people.

I take it all very seriously. I also provide a kind of after-service. I stay in touch with the people I put together so that if a problem arises they can come to me and we can work on it. I'm there as a back-up for them. For example, if the girl feels she wants out or he feels it's not right, I act as a kind of adviser. It's not just a 'take your money and go' affair.

There is an acute shortage of professional girls everywhere, even in Drogheda, Dundalk and Monaghan. That's the reason the Marese O'Shea Bureau came into being. The name of the original company was always EE, Exclusive Escorts. EuroEntertainment was another name for it. I was always conscious that the country customers were the ones who wanted a long-term relationship. I tested the water and discovered the need: I found that one out of every three customers wanted a longer involvement. It was a logical extension of the original dating agency to handle the needs of long-term customers. I would be there on the phone for hours introducing people. There were no computers used. I knew my girls and I soon learned which of them was the most suitable for a particular customer. People think it's just a matter of introducing an escort to a guy. It's not like that at all: people have to be really compatible for it to be successful. Sometimes I would meet customers but usually a good detailed talk on the phone was enough. Then there were other opportunities, the Christmas parties, for example.

It meant quite a lot of work. I had to manage upwards of seventy-five girls, thousands of customers, advertising and publicity. I used to type all the letters myself. I really earned any money I made and from time to time I would escort a customer myself. As soon as I earned it, though, it all went to feed my extravagant tastes. Ridiculous as it may seem, I saved nothing, invested nothing. I was still drinking and doing cocaine on and off. And then I had the guy with the children living in my luxurious flat. I had beautiful cars and gorgeous clothes. I wouldn't think twice about spending a couple of hundred pounds on a bottle of champagne, never thinking about tomorrow. I think my adoptive father's early death and my brother drowning changed me dramatically; 'tomorrow may never come' was my motto. It's a very stupid rule to live by – not a thing for a rainy day. When I was in the gutter I didn't even have three pounds for cigarettes or food, that's how bad it got.

One way and another I sold a lot of newspapers for a lot of companies. If things were quiet they'd ring looking for a story and of course I'd have one. My timing was always good, like for the Christmas parties. I used to run these amazing Christmas parties. They were fantastic and the girls had a ball. They were real fun. I'd have about ten or fifteen carefully chosen girls and the male guests were carefully vetted too. The girls had to be picked so that they got on with each other too. Mostly the guests would already be known to each other.

We had French maids serving and the food would be by the very best caterers. There were certain customers who would say, 'I'm always interested in parties,' and I'd let them know. The papers wanted to know if I'd let them in on a party but that could have been a problem. A majority of the guests would be company executives, say the director and a couple of his assistants, and they'd all come together. They'd have no sense of embarrassment because they were sure that no one would spill the beans. However I have had wives on to me trying to check up. They'd ring and they'd ask about the agency. They would have got the name from the credit card but my companies were always registered as art foundations and therefore well covered. That was enough to explain the large amount on the credit-card bill. Human nature being what it is, I'm sure some of the guests and girls ended up in bed together. After any party there's always some scandal.

We used to organise stag parties on commission. They were usually a bit rowdier than the Christmas parties which were controlled by me. I wouldn't allow strippers, for example. A stag party would be a special order. I would get a limit from a customer and I would spend every penny of it. I know other companies would try to skimp but I never even thought of doing that. The budget might be five to ten thousand pounds and that would cover where the party was held, the cars, security, food, drink and the company. I began to arrange specials like that in 1991-92 and my customers were secure in that no one would know the venue. That was why I made sure that the papers were never allowed to get any information.

The *Sunday World* and I got on very well. If I had another kind of business I might cooperate with a different type of newspaper but the *Sunday World* for me was like a regular magazine to customers. It was exactly as I wanted it. People in this country who are interested in prostitution services like it because through it they find out the new places. This was the market I wanted to reach and I specifically went for it. On the world scene, through the *Herald Tribune* I was able to reach a quarter of a million customers who would know my number. The *Sunday World* worked very well for the home market; it kept potential customers up to date.

I had no official arrangements with any of the hotels but I would advise my customers to go to the porter and prepare him for the escort arriving. I got to know a lot of hotel porters privately and I used to pay them £25 for every customer. If you were staying in one of the major hotels some of the porters would be inclined to be helpful to visitors, especially if you were foreign. They knew my number and so did the a lot of taxi-men. If a taxi driver had a customer who asked where he should go he would direct him to me. If it worked out I'd give him £25.

I used radio and television as well for publicity. I even appeared on *Nighthawks*. My purpose was not crude advertising; I was constantly trying to drum it into people that my operation was not a 'Sex for Sale' agency; I lost my voice trying to tell people what it was really like. I was on with Jonathan Philbin Bowman and participated quite regularly with Chris Barry. It was through Chris Barry that

Shay Healy of *Nighthawks* got on to me. I was quite apprehensive about the response I'd get to that, how people would react on Irish television. I need not have worried; it went down well. In fact I didn't need any publicity. There was no shortage of customers, the name had become so well known.

13

TOYBOYS, DISCIPLINE AND DOMINATION

I always believed that all angles should be covered, except abuse of children and heavy physical stuff. It had always seemed to me that some Irish women could use my services too. I provided escorts for them in the same way as I did for the men. You can call them toyboys if you like. At the start of the 1990s there was a bit of unfortunate publicity because of the the stupidity of one woman. A young guy ripped her off to the tune of sixteen thousand pounds. He started blackmailing her and she paid him off with a cheque. When I heard about it – it got a lot of publicity as it was considered a national scandal – I thought to myself; I'm doing it for men so why not do it for women. Soon I had some very beautiful foreign guys working for me: a French guy and a German, Andreas (he's now back in Germany). There were also a lot of English guys; they were beautiful. I never used English girls – they were never popular with my customers – whereas Irish girls were excellent.

By 1991 I was employing about twelve guys, and their customers were similar to the male customers, inter-

national businesswomen, rich, married, all sorts. Male
models were popular and the customers were usually
aged from the middle thirties up, though I did have one
beautiful young girl who made use of the service. It was
the same with the men. I used to wonder why people who
seemed to have everything should need my services but
they do it for their own reasons. They go out with a
prostitute because they're not looking for anything else
but the company for that night. Professional escorts are
used to being with people and they know how to satisfy
whatever needs they sense.

I called the male part of the service Eurostuds. The
Sunday World used the story and because of the publicity
about the woman who had been blackmailed I couldn't
keep up with the demand. They were all young, gorgeous
looking guys who actually liked women and though the
customers made no comment I knew they were exactly
what they wanted. I had been successful with the men and
I was right about the female customers too. The guy who
drove me when I was in New York used to work with
women and though I never got involved with him that way
I found him attractive. I never dealt with any of my own
guys. I was too busy.

When I was recruiting, as you might say, I'd know the
minute I met a guy if he was going to be suitable. When I
put advertisements out I got loads of responses but most
of the guys were full of delusions and had the wrong
attitude completely. I even got responses from among our
own customers from men who were completely unsuit-
able. There was something about the right ones that I
would just sense, maybe even the way they'd attend to

my needs. Anyway I'd spend a lot of hours in their company before I'd give them a job. All of them were interviewed very thoroughly and if they weren't attentive to me in every way, even in ways I hadn't thought of, I would decide that they weren't good enough. The ones I accepted were excellent.

About half the guys I used were foreign. This was because the foreign guys were already trained to the business, whereas I had to train the Irish lads. Andreas, for instance, who was German, was one of the best. Also Mickail, who was French. The Continental guys were aware of the level of attention you had to pay to make a woman feel special. There was no place for any macho stuff, that much was certain. It was harder work for me putting guys out, and more worrying. Women clients were more exacting than men.

As publicity for Eurostuds I offered a prize of a night out with a toyboy on a radio chat show. The girl who won the date on the show admitted she had never been better wined and dined. The radio station was going to get them some little meal in a small restaurant but I said, 'This one is going to get the works. We'll do this the Marese O'Shea way!' So they had pre-dinner drinks in one of the hotels and the Shelbourne supplied the meal. Then they had entertainment and they were chauffeur-driven throughout. I was asked if they ended up in bed and I had to answer that I didn't know, that I didn't think so. The evening went well and it gave a hint of what it could be like but the main purpose was to have a bit of fun. The important thing was that the reputation of Marese O'Shea was as high as ever.

The toyboy side worked exactly the same way as the callgirl side. Customers would ring up, introductions were made, and the rest was the affair of the parties concerned. A lot of people would ring for couples as well. Sometimes the call would come from another couple or sometimes it would just be one person on their own, or they'd go out to a party together. I was continually being hassled to provide men and women for customers of the same sex. I am not gay and I didn't know the scene very well. I gave that part of the business to a gay escort but he couldn't handle it. It ended up that I would have to do it myself and I really didn't have the energy. I would do it only for certain special customers. When you think of it it's no great problem introducing a male to a male or a female to a female; it's much the same as for a male to a female; they're all the one to me. Yet I knew it was going to be another huge thing to handle and I couldn't carry it at that time. I just didn't have the time to be as dedicated to it as I was to the male/female side of things.

Another, older, woman supplied a specialised TV [transvestite] service. Customers would have to come for a full day and she would give them the full make-over – hair, waxing, eye make-up, nails, clothes she would make for them herself. She had rooms packed with racks of clothes and underwear. She also provided her customers with rooms for relaxing and chatting with other trans-vestites. She got them up to a high enough standard to parade in Ibiza Town where the world's best transvestites are. Here at home Hallowe'en was a good time for trans-vestites because they could go out quite comfortably at party time, as if in fancy dress.

I once brought a transvestite customer home. He pulled up on the street and asked if we could go back to my place. As we walked up the stairs to my flat I caught a glimpse of high heels and a dress under his coat. I was mortified in case any of my friends in the other flats spotted that he was a transvestite.

The business was booming; this empire was going up not brick by brick but wall by wall around me. I didn't think that it was going to become so powerful. I suppose I wanted power or at least some external security. It became an empire and it still is, it's still there. It's quiet at the moment, dormant even, which is very good for it and which gives it strength. I've temporarily sedated it and I suppose I still have the power to resuscitate it but I don't know if I would want to go back publicly. I no longer want a high profile. In fact I think I'd be jeopardising my life if I had that.

I used the word power and now that I think about it it does play an important part in my profession. Prostitutes, certainly successful ones, have a kind of power. I suppose that's why so many women take it up as a career; it's not just the money. For the first time, I suppose, they have men, usually the bosses, in their hands, almost at their mercy. That's the way it was for me anyway. If a guy wanted to be with me I had the choice: I could say yes or no.

Since starting psychotherapy I've thought a lot about the work I do and people's motivation in prostitution, both the girls' and the customers'. Power plays its part and so does revenge. It may not be very strong or even a conscious thing but I think some women in the business have scores to settle and they do this by exploiting the vulnerability of men. I can give you an illustration of this, though I did not fully realise its significance until it happened to me, after I went to Coolmine. I was walking to the shop one day with another girl and we were passing by a pub in Clonee. It was a beautiful day and as we were walking by this car pulls in. I knew it was a customer; I could tell even from a distance. I'm so used to working on the street that I can recognise a customer at a distance. It was just a quick glance between this man and myself. He was driving into the pub and we had stopped to let him in. By the time he had parked, we were still walking by the wall. He got out and he spoke. I said, 'Sorry?' and he said, 'I said it was a beautiful day. Do you want to go for a drink?' When I came back and recounted the incident to the staff, it emerged that this kind of thing had happened to several of them.

I said something like, 'I must have a label on me.' But the reality was that the man was vulnerable and I saw the vulnerability in him. If I had gone for that drink I could have taken advantage of that vulnerability. He wanted more than company; he wanted a female in every way. And that need made him defenceless. That particular man had what I used to call the look. It was so easy to recognise. It spoke of a kind of hunger and a belief that a particular woman could satisfy it. This look used to really bug me all my life. I'd be with a boyfriend and I'd see a certain look between him and another woman. I'd see eye contact and know what it meant.

It's a certain look which means so much though no words are spoken. I've done it myself and the next minute you could look at the person again and that look isn't there. It's like a connection, a chemistry. I could never understand that look until that day with the man in Clonee. Its characteristic is its openness, its vulnerability. With other people you see their looks mean nothing. You just look away because nothing has happened. Yet when it does happen it's unmistakable. Not everybody shows it but with the vulnerable people it's there. I suppose it is a sign that I'm beginning to understand relationships at last.

That kind of look that I would see flash between a boyfriend and another woman used to worry me a lot. It might seem a very small thing but it was big to me and it would cause a major problem that night. I would say, 'Why the eye contact? There must be more to it.' I was abnormally susceptible to worrying about it. I'd ponder on it and make a big deal out of it. It meant to me that his needs were not being met. I couldn't fulfil them; I wasn't even fulfilling my own.

At that time I did not normally take customers myself but a couple of times I made an exception. Guys would pressurise me to meet them, public names, and so to escape from the misery at home I agreed. Maybe too I felt the need to exercise a bit of power. I certainly liked the feeling of being out with powerful people. These were public figures and they were taking risks. They would take me to meet their friends or to their houses when their wives were out. I recall one guy in particular, a powerful businessman. We found we were into the same things; we both liked drugs and the jetset life. So we'd go off partying together, living the high life. This guy in particular would get a kick out of us doing the business in his car, which he used to park in the road right at the back of his house – in a neighbourhood where he was very well known. I used to be be terrified that someone would see us. At other times men like him would go to my apartment when I was living on my own.

I'm sure the other residents of apartment blocks where I lived were never aware of what was going on. I was discreet, even if the customers weren't. These VIP customers would often have a bodyguard and he'd have to take a walk during the operation. I'd always dress in a fur coat with lingerie under it. Once or twice I was asked if I'd mind if the bodyguard joined in. That was when things really got out of hand, when I was heavily into drugs. Sometimes, however, it was fun. There were men I went out with and I found them so fascinating I would ignore the money. People say you wouldn't be with them if they didn't have the cash but they're not quite right. Some of these men had such interesting personalities that they would make you want to come anyway. They knew how to have a good time themselves although I knew the problems of every single one of them.

I had one of the most marvellous nights of my life with my Irish rock star; he was beautiful. I went so deep in there. People like him – well, their life is on the line in public and that can be really frightening. This guy had me collected by a driver and brought to his place. I could have been some crazy person; yet he knew that he could trust me. That was because my agency was built on security and its reputation was good. In the past I had provided escorts for him for parties. There would regularly be rock parties when the stars would come into

Dublin – actors or other rock stars. This happened often when Irish rock stars would entertain foreign ones. They'd have these big parties and I'd supply some of the women and they knew that the girls I'd be sending out would be gorgeous. There would also be women they'd found for themselves but I think they were safer with the company they bought because they knew these girls weren't after them for who they were. They knew there'd be no follow-up. They wouldn't be hounded; they were safe. Sometimes in situations like that it's better to pay for escorts.

Politicians are a different ballgame. They can be peculiar. I used to meet one of them regularly in a really seedy parlour. This guy used often to come into me, trying to disguise himself, but you'd spot him. He'd a scarf wrapped around him and these big glasses but he'd a very prominent feature and it really showed no matter what he did. He took some risks and he was horrible to look after as regards his fetishes. It didn't do anything for me and I disliked a lot of it. The only saving grace was that the girls and I used to have great fun with him. He'd spend four or five hours in the parlour and he used to love being tied up. We'd pretend to go up and burn him; we wouldn't in fact but we'd pretend to and of course this really turned him on. He liked clothes pegs put on his nipples. He was a tough customer to look after. We used to take turns because he'd be there for hours and between other customers we'd nip in and we'd all play our part. He wasn't a great payer, incidentally.

Whenever there were several of us on the job the crack was good and the customers liked it too. We had one politician, a regular, whose pleasure was to be a slave. He was great; he'd do anything for you. He'd ring every day and ask for me. This was when I was on my own. I knew him from the parlour days but then he came to me when he knew I was in private practice. Every morning he would ring me and ask did I have messages I wanted done. He would do anything for me. He'd clean the apartment if I needed it. If I wanted a cream cake he'd go miles to get it; he was great.

Politicians sometimes used the state cars. One in particular frequented a parlour in town. The driver of the state car would check the road and drive a couple of times around the block to make sure that the coast was clear. He'd ring up then and say, 'Have the door open now!' and he'd jump out just outside the parlour. I changed all that. I would arrange beautiful, private, isolated premises for them to go to. The accommodation would be in country houses but they would be like mini-castles. I found this fantastic outfit that did really exclusive properties. You could book for a weekend or even a night. You might book it for a week and use it only for a night. I'd never use the same place twice. No one, including the customer, would know where they were going till they got there. Even the driver was in the dark except for getting directions, of course. That's what total security means; they could trust me.

The thing is that all my VIP customers whether politicians, big businessmen, rock stars or actors were more or less alike. In the acting and the rock world I did find them more drug-oriented, but politicians and other professional people who were in the public eye would also be into drugs or drink. It was just a different way of doing it. I must say too that I liked most of them and remained friends with all but a few. Whenever I do feel tempted to fall for men I think of the two mad passionate relationships that were a disaster – the man who took me to America and the guy with the five children.

I was always well dressed and I was young and pretty. I soon found out that these things weren't all that important. I mean they were important for me but not all that essential for the customers. You learn very quickly that there's really no accounting for people's tastes, especially when you're a prostitute. Men like variety. There is no kind of woman who will not please somebody. Women who have a lot of weight can turn men on. There is no set shape but I suppose a standard figure would be the normal preference. I wouldn't have anyone grossly overweight in any of my operations.

Appearance, age and shape are important but not crucial. What is crucial is the impression that is made. First impressions last. I knew this very beautiful, elegant lady with a great figure and good clothes. Yet customers would go to her once and never go back. She couldn't hold a customer by her personality. She had a very cold attitude, and prostitution goes a lot deeper than sex. The sex is at the very end; it's the personality, the company, that brings customers back. The only type of customer who would want a woman as cold as that would be one who was into fantasy. They might like a woman who was cold; deliberately unfriendly and frigid.

Customers want so many different things; it depends on the guy and how he feels at the time. Usually customers come in with the world's troubles on their shoulders and the last thing they want is a girl who's going to be talking about her problems. They want someone with a cheerful outlook. There is no simple answer; there are a lot of things that a customer looks for. You can't just say any one thing. A girl who's chatty and who enjoys her work is usually the number one. The word prostitution is wrong, it really is, because it confines the business to sex and in fact for most people the company is so much more important. You can have two women, one doing it when she doesn't want to be and shouldn't be, and she takes it out on a customer. That is what a customer doesn't need but gets quite a lot. The other is cheerful and good company and gives the impression of enjoying what she does. She is likely to be assertive and give the impression that she herself has chosen it as a career. The customers who come through me would never be subjected to an unwilling, grumpy prostitute.

Sometimes you meet really nasty types. I've been in a few situations like that, where I just had to leave because it was so horrible being abused verbally or physically. This might sound disgusting but there are ways of having sex and being abused at the same time. Once I said to a customer, 'There's your money; I don't need money that badly.' Most men are decent enough but I'd say about a third are horrible. I put those into a category of people with problems and they take them out on prostitutes; they look on prostitutes as not being real people.

At times customers wanted to act out fantasies and you had to help to bring out these fantasies, to create fantasies, making them a reality. There were certain fantasies that I wouldn't entertain, like a lot of child stuff.

I had a problem with it.

Exclusive Escorts always had the best; for example when it came to discipline we had the Domination Queen. She was in her late forties, a tall, thin, severe-looking woman who always seemed very angry. She loved to take her anger out on the customers, which was exactly what they wanted. Even as they arrived, she'd be beating them in the door. She insisted on punctuality and customers would be 'punished' if they arrived late. Of course they would deliberately be late in order to provoke her anger. Then she would send them on messages and they would be severely punished for the slightest misdemeanour. She had every imaginable device – whips, canes, leather pieces, wooden pieces. She had her house (which she bought on the proceeds of working for Exclusive Escorts) kitted out with chains and leads and handcuffs and a barrel to lock customers in. She even had a dungeon built to lock them up. She'd use a dog-collar and lead them around the room. They'd have to plead with her, calling her 'Mistress', kissing her feet, catering to her every whim, really debasing themselves. I did domination myself but I wasn't a patch on the Domination Queen. She seemed really to enjoy it and to be downright vicious.

Guys would come in and they'd offer amazing money in order for me to cane them. But if they wanted to cane *me* I'd always say, 'No way, never!' When I was working the street there was one guy – I don't know why it was but I trusted him, probably because he was well known publicly and I figured he wouldn't go to town on me – who offered me £10 for every time he'd cane me. He ended up giving me £100 a session. This was good money, although I couldn't sit down for a while. Still I earned a day's pay with one customer! I met him on Waterloo Road. He pulled up in a gorgeous sportscar and was obviously very wealthy. I decided for once to be practical and say yes. He came back for more; I still talk to him to this day as a friend. He was a special case, though; I did make an exception for him and I have continued to do so. I've never let any other customer do it.

I know what can happen with sadistic stuff because I've heard so many girls say, 'The guy started hitting me and went to town on me.' But then you're back to the situation where the customers aren't vetted, where someone off the street can just come over and attack girls. That didn't happen to me but I was there while two guys were attacking girls in Thomas Street. Vetting is very important because men ask a lot for discipline. A lot of guys like it and also the reverse, domination, being humiliated and that. But it can be very dangerous and needs a lot of control.

In spite of what is generally believed, only about half the customers are married and a fair number of them are young. At times I have refused guys who are too young. Sometimes older men will come and bring younger guys with them. I suppose they are fathers with sons or uncles with nephews. There are quite a lot of young guys from eighteen up, but the average age would be from around forty to fifty. The married customers would be ones who do not want to have affairs and who say they treasure their marriages. They don't want them to break up. But they feel they have needs that must be satisfied. The experience seems to help them; it gives them a boost if they're with somebody new. I'm not married but I can imagine that being with the one partner day in day out, week after week, year after year, must get a bit boring. I'm not speaking about all marriages but a lot of husbands find their way to people like me.

I was always amazed by the number of high-profile people, including actors, television personalities, businessmen and politicians, who were using the services of a prostitute, since they ran such a risk of being caught.

Some male customers when they rang up, even at the first call, would have a kind of menu of exactly what they wanted. They would specify the colour of hair, eyes, the shape of her nose, neck – the lot, right down to her toes. They indicated exactly what they would like, a rounded bottom or one that stuck out; they really went into detail. When the kind of girl was settled they'd then say what their sexual preferences were, whether they were into feet or nails or humiliation or whatever. I'd have girls that were experts in all these areas. The majority would not know what they wanted and in that case I had some girls who were experts at discovering what a particular customer really preferred. I can do it myself when I am long enough with a man. There are loads of ways of testing. The guy might be bisexual and not even know it. That has happened loads of times. It's just a matter of playing games with the customer and from these games finding out by his reactions what are his real sexual preferences. His body might be saying, 'Yes I'm into that,' and in his head he's trying to contradict it. It is by the body's reaction that you learn the truth.

A latent bisexual might go for a girl who has a boyish

appearance. For that reason I used to be very popular when I worked because I had very small breasts and I think a lot of them used to fantasise about me in that way. They do go by the figures. Others might be turned on by a resemblance to a friend or acquaintance: if the girl looks like someone they know – it could be just from a glance, a look that would remind them of a situation – the sexual drive will increase. With sexual fantasies, anything that works at the time is what turns them on. As I have always said, so long as the fantasies are not centred on children, which I can't abide, and not too physically violent, I see no harm in them and always had that as the basic principle of my operation. When I was with the customers I knew ones who were dangerous. There were certain customers that I was frightened of because their behaviour was too close to the line. There were others and you'd just know by them that their fix wouldn't lead to anything serious.

Some men go to prostitutes because they want to feel that they are attractive to women, especially if they have not had much success in that line. When they go to a prostitute they do want her to enjoy the sex and are prepared to pay extra for her to enjoy it. As I said in an earlier chapter, from the time I decided to work I made the rule that I would never climax when I was with a customer. This attitude sprang from the fear of enjoying myself so much with a customer that maybe I wouldn't have pleasure with my partner. I have known it to happen as some prostitutes are highly sexed. A lot of prostitutes, well a few, have become lesbians. They came into the business having relationships with men and then turned to women. Maybe those feelings were already there and when they were in the business they met other lesbians.

You find that when you're working as a prostitute you need lots of love because you're giving away so much of yourself. You just need to be wrapped up and cherished afterwards but you don't get much of that. A lot of girls have men they go home to, husbands or partners, but all of us are left after work with a build-up of feelings that need to be soothed. Sometimes you can get comfort from the customers. I've often been held and felt loved by customers. You really need cherishing because you're very vulnerable after working, wide open. Most times prostitutes choose to keep these feelings secret. They want to make sure that no one knows they're working and they bottle all their feelings up inside. That's what destroys people and makes them turn to things like drugs.

14

FINDING MY MOTHER AND FATHER

In 1992 I was nearly thirty-two and had a very successful escort agency, loads of money and a big apartment. Yet things were very bad. I was still burdened with the crook and his five children and I had started going out with some of the very well known customers myself. I think it was a way to escape from the situation I was living in. I was going with the big customers, doing cocaine and spending nights out. Then I got the letter to say that contact had been made with my birth mother.

I had been looking for her for years. I'd wanted to find her from when I was eleven or twelve. The interest was there and it was just a natural thing to want to know who she was. I suppose the main stimulus was simple curiosity. I had my baptismal certificate so I knew I had been baptised in a church in Blackrock and I had been in Temple Hill orphanage there. When I was about twenty I rang the parish priest out there. I was entitled to the name, he said. He asked me my given name and I told him Louise Finn. He was able to tell me my biological mother's name, which was written beside mine in the register. The first thing I did was look up the phone book to see if the name with her initials was printed there and of course it wasn't. When I did find her, I learned that she was from Dublin's inner city.

As I have already mentioned, for years I used to drink in an inner-city pub where all the gangsters used to go. I'd try and make it every night for the last drink because I used to a get a sense of belonging there and it was the only place I ever felt that. Little did I know that some of the guys I met in there, who became mates, whom I'd go out and have meals with, go out drinking with, were relatives of my own. When eventually I found my mother, at our second meeting she told me that some of these friends were my first cousins. I nearly died because I'd been going out with them. I was shocked.

My politician friend told me I should go to Barnardo's. They advised me to go to the adoption board in D'Olier House, which I did. I gave them the name I had and all I knew, which wasn't much. I was put in touch with the St Gabriel's Adoption Agency in Haddington Road. When I rang there they advised that I go into them for counselling. The building is just a house now but it's still like a convent inside. I went in and spoke to the counsellor. There were certain important things she said to me: she prepared me for the possibility of my mother not wanting to meet me, so I was ready for that.

The counsellor prepared me in other ways I hadn't thought of. She told me a number of important things and left them with me. I went off and thought about them. I was in Merrion Court and things were still flying: the guy with the children was still there; I was still torn apart about my own daughter; there was articles about me in the paper; there were radio shows and loads of other things going on. About six weeks after my visit to St Gabriel's I got a letter from them saying that they had been in touch with my mother and, yes, she did want to meet me. I was overwhelmed. But all the thoughts I had of what our first meeting might be like were wrong. The day I went to meet her for the first time and I walked into that room I felt so cold when I saw her.

We met in St Gabriel's – it's the usual practice. I learned very quickly that I had seven half-brothers and sisters; my sisters, three of them, were in the pub across the road while my mother was with me. My own daughter was with me as well, although I was on my own at the introduction. I imagined it was going to be an affectionate meeting. My mother did come over and put her arms around me and I froze. This wasn't pre-planned; it happened instinctively; I just froze. I didn't realise then but I do now after my therapy in Coolmine that really I was very angry and very hurt. Naturally the first question I put to her was: 'Why did you give me up?' and she gave me a cock-and-bull story about her father. The second thing I said to her was that I worked as a prostitute. I think I was trying to hurt her. My thinking was crazy; it was so childish. The damage I did to her was unfair because I hurt her badly and she really did try. She welcomed me into her home and my sisters did their best to welcome me.

She did her best to be friendly; she told her other children about me, which she didn't need to do. I discovered from her that she hadn't married my father. She had the seven children in her own marriage but she was separated. I found my father later. I think she had a hard life. The meeting was quite severe on me and I'm sure it was no fun for her either. I asked her if she had ever held me as a baby and she said no. In the place where I was born on Ranelagh Road all the babies were kept at the top of the house and she sneaked up one night – the mothers weren't allowed to go up – and that was the only glance she got. I didn't like hearing all this. I wasn't ready for it: I was drinking very heavily at the time and I could sense that my mother didn't approve of the business I had.

I started calling into her house. In time she told me my father's name and where he worked so I phoned him. He didn't come from the the inner city; he's quite different from my mother but he is an alcoholic. As a person, my mother is very soft and tender although she has lived a very hard life, whereas my father is totally extrovert, travelling the world a lot, mad into rare books – but a mess. When I rang he said he knew me. I didn't even have to say who I was. I said his name on the phone and he said 'I know who you are,' and he said my mother's name. 'You're her daughter.' I said, 'Would you like to meet?' He said, 'I've been waiting for you to ring.'

I discovered that my mother had been seventeen when I was born, the same age as I was when I had Catherine. My father was about the same age so he hadn't really been able or willing to take any responsibility. He didn't want to marry my mother but later on he did marry and I've three brothers and a sister on that side. He was still with his wife though the marriage wasn't great – living in the same house but pretending. He arranged to meet me that week but I was drinking a lot and I didn't make it. He rang me, I rang him back and arranged to meet him in Blanchardstown.

I told him that I was a prostitute when I met him. He said, 'I'm so sorry that it turned out that way.' I wasn't very impressed when he said that. He lives very close to my adopted family on the Navan Road and he was drinking in the pubs that I was drinking in all my life. I actually knew my half-brothers on my father's side. I was lifted up on one of their shoulders at a U2 concert. Apparently my sister looks like me. I haven't met her but I gather she's a mess, crazy. Some of my brothers are away, living abroad. I didn't ever meet my father's wife.

I was down in my local pub one night, this was before I went into Coolmine for the first time, and he was there drinking. He asked me to come up to the house and I said I wouldn't go to his wife's house. He said that she was away and started working on me: 'Are you afraid of me?' – that sort of thing. I felt like when I was being abused as a kid, not wanting to do it. I didn't like that. I went with him and he made me a sandwich. He was urging me to stay but I didn't trust him. We were alone and I just didn't feel safe staying there. So I got a taxi even though I'd no money.

Not long afterwards, his daughter's boyfriend approached me in the local pub and disgraced me, roaring, 'Go back to your drugs! You're not wanted in the family.' The guy's not even in the family. My father wanted to meet me, and it's none of the business of any of his children what he does. I knew them before I knew he was my father. The daughter is the problem; she's the one who has difficulty with the set-up. Her boyfriend was really crazy; he started calling up to my friend's house shouting, 'Come out, Louise Finn!' It was probably the way their father dealt with it. I rang him after Coolmine, to see if he would meet me. I was really hurt when he said he didn't want to.

Even though you can be very hurt I do recommend that adopted children try to meet their biological parents. It is a natural thing to want to know something about your origins. However, before people do take the step I would strongly advise them to think about it as much as they can. They should consider their own lives, try to analyse their feelings and understand their motives for starting the search. They should be ready for disappointment because it's a lot to take. You really have to be forearmed emotionally.

Before I met my biological mother my life had got to such a stage that I was in danger of getting into drugs again. On one occasion I suffered a toxic reaction because I'd taken some tablets that a guy I knew gave me when I went down looking for some hash one night. This guy down in Belvedere Place had no hash so he said to me, 'Here's some tablets.' Drug addict that I was, I took them. He said to me, '*One* of them! Be careful.' One night I just took the whole lot together. My body wouldn't stop shaking and I couldn't talk. It was like having an epileptic fit that went on for days. It was very frightening: my mind understood what was going on but my body couldn't get it together.

Eventually I came to but my body didn't. I had to have injections in my spine. I was put on an opiate and that started me back looking for heroin again. I was running the business from my bed. I had my mattress brought into the front room with three phones and two lines on each beside me. Girls were still going all around the country, the business was as big as ever. My voice began to go and eventually I lost it completely. I wasn't eating and I went down to about five stone. In the mornings I'd have to make sure the girls were on the train or had their drivers, and that their accommodation was ready.

The Dublin operation was still going on and Europe was thriving, and all of these things had to be sorted out before ten in the morning, before I came on the air. The radio shows were inviting me on to speak. I was in my bed and my life was falling apart. I ended up in hospital and I just had to close the phones down for a couple of weeks. That guy was still with me but his children ended up back home with their mother. She took them back after she broke up with her boyfriend. I ended up going back home to my mother's house and your man came with me, believe it or not. I was very ill; I had no energy to do anything. The business was back in action so I would be taking my breakfast and the phone would ring. While I answered it the food would go cold and be left uneaten. It was all so stupid. Eventually the relationship with the guy who had the five children came to an end – and not before time.

15

KISSING COUSINS

I always knew that looking for my parents could be risky. I didn't realise just what it would cost me or them. I soon discovered that two of my mother's sons, my half-brothers, were drug addicts. One is now clean after a lot of hard work and he's doing really well. The other is younger and he is still on drugs. It's very sad and I'm sure my mother is broken-hearted. My coming along didn't help. She said she'd thought about me. For two years she was waiting for me to come along and when I do I'm a mess and drinking a lot. And then I fall in love with her nephew and we both end up on heroin. I came along and I hurt her. I did the classic thing I was always doing, hurting people in order to hurt myself, keeping a distance, pushing her away. I did it with everybody. It was a pattern of behaviour I had learned when I was very young, and when the time came I did it with my mother as well.

The thing is she's so homely that I'd love a relationship with her. I feel I've so much to give. But when I fell in love with her nephew our behaviour hurt her very badly. My mother has six or seven sisters and they're all homely.

One of these aunts, the mother of a guy I knew from the pub, had a party for me at Christmas for the purpose of introducing me to all the family. The younger people were upstairs and this particular cousin came down. I was sitting on a chair and he took me by the hand to take me upstairs and it was from that moment I knew that I loved him. The next thing we were kissing each other and we ended up together.

It was without a doubt one of the great love affairs of my life and it was all the more intense and deep for me because I'd been looking for my blood relatives for so long. There is even a marking on our skin that we both have, though in different places. Little things like that made me feel even closer to him. He really introduced me to the family. I would never have got to know them the way I did if it hadn't been for him. He was introducing me to cousins and relatives all over the place. I really felt he cared for me. I had the business still so I left my mother's house in Castleknock and moved with my cousin to a flat on North Great George's Street.

It was strange to fall for a man whom I already knew as a friend and then rediscovered as a cousin. When I met him first I was around twenty-five and he was about seven years younger than me. I suppose I was ready for affection at the time. The Christmas party was only a few months after I finally got shut of the guy with the children. From the moment our hands touched at that party I knew he was the one for me. Immediately we kissed in front of all his family. My friend John grabbed me by the arm and pulled me out of the house but the next day my cousin rang me and we met again.

He was just back from America and he'd had a cocaine habit over there which he kicked when he came back here. He had ventured into harder drugs, and I was the same. I was years and years off heroin but I was still taking other drugs. When we met the two of us just went straight into the heroin. It was Christmas and we said, 'Will we have a smoke?' I'd cut off all communication with every drug dealer I ever knew but he was from town and knew everyone who was involved with drugs. He had tried heroin but he wasn't strung out on it.

I don't blame my cousin for my addiction. I got myself back into heroin. The two of us were in it together; we fell in love while we were getting high on heroin. At the beginning you get a high but that goes very quickly and it turned out that eventually we were killing each other for the drug. It took over everything we had; all our feelings went. Eventually we even lost our feelings for each other and for ourselves.

Some weeks would be incredible. The agency would be totally booked up, making thousands. I recall spending up to four thousand pounds a week on heroin eventually. I was keeping two habits going then, my own and my cousin's, and I had a cocaine habit as well. Anyway, even if I had been clean and had four thousand pounds for myself I would have found a way to spend it. When I was in Coolmine my counsellor asked me to write down what I was spending my money on. It was the first time I'd done it. I was spending say, two thousand on food and bills and four on heroin. That was frightening. She said to me, 'Go back and see for yourself what you spent your money on.' I could not believe it. Then I was adding up two habits, using six hundred pounds a day between the two of us. It's not hard to do because, when your habit is big, no matter how much you have you just keep taking more and more.

I wouldn't be looking at it like that. I was only thinking of the need to have the largest possible quantity of heroin instead of this going around for twenty pounds-worth at a time. Sometimes there'd be scarcities and you'd spend your days driving around until you got it. The more we had the more we'd use and the more money you have the bigger your habit gets. You buy it in bulk when you can get it. There were some dealers who always had it but then you'd get certain areas where the younger guys would sell batches for the main dealer. If they sold ten little bags they got four for themselves for free; that's how most of them support their habit.

The cops took me in once for a drugs search but because my cousin had a business they didn't suss that we were addicts. Yet we'd be talking to every addict on the street because everybody knows everybody else. You'd bump into them when you were scoring [buying]. Now that I think about it I cannot believe that some things actually happened: knocking on dealers' doors, asking: 'Have you got anything?' You wouldn't see the madness of it when you needed something. I'd sit for hours in the freezing cold a bit back from a block of flats just waiting to see a supplier. At least if I had been working the street I'd have made some money.

The guards can't really do much because there are just so many people strung out out there, thousands. Being an addict means you have to get up and steal while you're sick because you've taken drugs and you need more. You have to get out of bed sick to go out and rob. I can't see the guards ever cleaning up the addicts. All that's happened now, especially in town, is that they've moved out a little bit further.

When my cousin and I were clean, totally clean and not drinking, it was beautiful together. So our love affair wasn't drug-induced; it was real. But for two addicts together it was only a matter of time. One day I'd be strong and he'd be weak and then one day the two of us were weak and we were hooked on heroin again. Things got a lot worse but we went on for a year or two. Then I ended up in Coolmine and I stayed! It was over by then. We split up before I went into Coolmine the second time, things had got so bad.

I admire my cousin still today for his determination and his strength. He'd make a decision and he'd stand by it. He is an upholsterer and he opened up his own business with my help. When I came on the scene he was getting the dole and hadn't any capital. Financially, I let him use me as a stepping stone. He managed it himself but I do feel I aided him in getting to where he is and he deserves it. The business is successful. He's drinking, though. I suppose he needs some release. Even at the worst times he has managed to hold it together, although barely, and with help from his brothers. They're upholsterers as well; it's in the family. He had great support from the family. His elder brother is clean now and he's doing very well. His mother and father were wonderful and I envied him that because I had no one that cared for me the way they cared for him. I felt angry about it.

Something I feel quite hurt about is the fact that his

family blamed me for him taking drugs. He'd been experimenting with drugs long before he met me. My aunt made a lot of very hurtful remarks. OK, we shouldn't have been together in the first place, and together we would never have got clean. We knew that ourselves but they made me out to be the one responsible. I say it again: I didn't get him on drugs; he was well into drugs before I met him. Nor did he get *me* into them. We're two separate people.

Towards the end of the affair I found out that he was deceiving me. When we were living in North Great George's Street he had sex with his younger brother's girlfriend in the bathroom while I was asleep in bed. It wasn't I who discovered it but I knew something had happened. His brother told me that his girlfriend had said it. He lied to me and kept denying it. He lied for a week and then it came out. So the trust went. He had given me a little ornamental house with our surnames on it when we met the first time; it was a little cottage, like an Irish pub. During a row he smashed it. It meant the world to me and when it was smashed that was the beginning of the end.

He was a wizard as regards managing money. I have no sense of it at all and if I have it I spend it. I live well if I can on what money I have and if I don't have it I do without it. With him it was: if you have money, hold on to it. Minimise your spending. I'd go out and spend £10 on a piece of fillet steak and he'd say, you'd get a dinner for £3. This was the difference between us. He'd lived a different life from mine. Of course economy meant nothing anyway when I was spending thousands of pounds on heroin. He always told me that he didn't love me and yet I've cards at home that say, 'I love you'. But I don't think he loved me the way I loved him.

My cousin-lover had just split up with a Spanish girl when I met him. He was attractive to women. I suppose he was one of these guys who have no trouble in getting partners. He's with another woman now. He was the type who eyed other women when we were out together. One serious problem was that I couldn't have children and he really wanted to have his own child. It was a major difficulty. That was when it really hit me: *I can't have children.* I knew that I was going to have to let him go because of this. I found that very hard to take on board; it hurt so much.

Such hassle wasn't what I needed at the time. There were a lot of problems as well with my adoptive mother and my daughter. He'd say, 'Your daughter is taking your mother's side.' He was right: she used to turn my daughter against me. He was quite frank about it. When my mother died and left the house to my daughter and I said it to him, the first thing he said was, 'I told you.' It wasn't that simple. I was on drugs at the time she changed the will and she was probably afraid I'd go and spend it on drugs – which I probably would have! I would have left everything to my daughter anyway. I know my adoptive mother didn't have a perfect way of rearing a child but she did her best. She did more than his aunt did: this woman reared me.

His aunt, my own mother, did not approve. She said to me when I told her, 'Your very own cousin . . . ' But he was like a stranger to me. There seemed to be no more to it than there was between me and my adoptive cousins.

This 'very own cousin' was really no more than a pub acquaintance before we got together. It caused a rift but it was mild compared to her response to the drugs. She just didn't want to know and I can't blame her. She called around to the flat one time. It was open-plan and the bedroom was up in the loft. You could look over into the living space. I could see her there and she didn't know that he was living with me. She went to go upstairs and he had to hide under the bed. She didn't approve of the business I was in, either. I hadn't any money from it at the time; it was all going on drugs.

My cousin insisted that I give up working as a prostitute myself. I found him quite old-fashioned; I think he wanted me to go into a nine-to-five job. He would have liked me suddenly to change my life but it wasn't going to happen. He did support me when I'd be up to my eyes. He helped me as much as he could but he was interfering in my life. He put me down by referring to the business all the time and knocking me as a person. Maybe it was because I was a prostitute, I don't know.

16

STRUNG OUT

My cousin and I spent all our time going around after drugs and he was very cruel to me towards the end. For a year he hadn't earned any money and I was the sole provider. He did help when he could but he was in the pub with his friends quite a lot and I always made sure that his pocket was never empty. He started complaining that the phone was ringing too often and annoying him. It was just that he didn't want me running the business from the flat. I gradually stopped, turning the phone off when he was there. Business was getting quieter and quieter. I pulled my ads and spent my time taking heroin instead.

We spent all day getting heroin. If it wasn't good we'd get more; if it *was* good we'd get more. So I was either asleep or he'd be there and the phone would be off and the business was going downhill. It was a really hard year. The girls kept asking, 'Where are you?' They were relying on me but life was becoming more difficult and the drugs were getting stronger as well. We never actually mainlined [injected into a vein] but we certainly smoked. He would always say, 'No! Not the needle!' but what we were doing was just as bad.

The longer you smoke, the less you end up getting out of it, so sometimes people think it's cheaper to inject. It's true that at the start you need a smaller amount in your vein to get the hit, but inevitably you need more. Smoking, or 'chasing the dragon' as it's called, means that you put the heroin powder on tinfoil and heat it. Then you make a tube out of the foil and the heroin runs and you suck it in. It's a quick smoke, not like a cigarette. You'd take the line and leave it for a bit to see how you feel. The sweat would start disappearing and you'd begin to relax. Sometimes you'd take the whole thing; people do it in different ways.

The first time I tried to kick heroin was horrific. I was back living at home because I was trying to get clean. I had to go to the National Drugs Centre in Pearse Street to give a urine sample. I had no money; I didn't even have the bus fare to get in there. My health was very poor. It's part of the illness I'm still living with, but at the time I thought it was entirely as a result of the drugs. I don't know how I survived. My mother would keep increasing the level of the central heating because the cold I felt was terrible. I'll never forget that cold. She'd keep arguing while I was trying to keep my head.

I managed to stay off drugs long enough to get into Coolmine the first time. I remember I arrived there on a Friday night and on the Saturday the lodge where the men live went on fire and they all had to come and stay in the girls' house. They were all sleeping downstairs. I only stayed a couple of weeks but I remember every second I spent there. But I got a letter from my cousin asking me to come back. He had started going to Narcotics Anonymous. Catherine brought me the letter but did not realise what she was doing. I was the one who took it from her, I was the dishonest one; she didn't know. She was only fifteen at the time. I believed my cousin when he said that he was clean, that he was running his business very well – and that he missed me.

I suppose to be honest the letter was not the only reason I left. The place was very strict at the time. The system worked and saved many people's lives but I looked for every excuse to leave. And I finally convinced myself that I had to go because I wanted to be with my daughter. I was just playing games, I know that now. To go into Coolmine and leave before they advise you, thinking that you can go back into society and not take drugs, is crazy.

Because of the fire the men were down in the women's section and the male staff were down in Ashleigh House in Clonee as well. They are amazing people. I was fascinated and I wanted to go back and learn more. I can't talk in detail about it because what you see and hear you leave there but it opened my mind. I wanted more and I knew I'd go back. Still I left, saw my cousin again and we started going out together. We tried to stay clean but we got bored very soon. One night we went to a concert in the Olympia Theatre and ended up taking drugs. We were back the next morning again. A couple of months later my cousin was blaming me for taking drugs and for starting him again. That's when I went to Italy with my daughter for a week.

I stayed off drugs. I took an amount of physeptone and

methadone and I sweated it out. I went through it and came back clean. I rang him before I came back and he said he was off the drugs and the night I came back he collected me at the airport. I wanted to be with him so I really tried. He drove me home and I said, 'Will we go out to a club and have a drink?' and he said, 'Well I'm meeting a guy at twelve o'clock but you don't have to take it.' But I was an addict so it was straight back on the heroin again. A friend of his lent him his flat for the night and we had a nice night together on heroin. I thought that even if I took it that night I'd be OK as long as I didn't take it the next morning. Of course the next morning we went straight off to get more, back into the old habits again. So that was a waste of a week in Italy.

We ended up moving into a flat together on the North Circular Road. We stayed there four or five months, our habits getting worse daily. My business was really fizzling out; my phone was never switched on and the girls and customers couldn't get me. My cousin was getting fed up of me because our habit was getting worse and I wasn't making any money.

I went home, closed down the agency and gave up the phone line. There was nowhere else for me to go but back on the street.

17

BACK ON THE STREET

That was how I ended up back working the street on Fitzwilliam Square in 1994-95. There was no point in trying to run the business any longer so I contacted as many people as I could to let them know. A lot of the customers didn't know what had happened, and were wondering where I had gone.

Going back on the street was hard. I hadn't been there since I had the apartment in Clanwilliam Court at the beginning of 1990. Then, too, I was regarded as very select and could afford to be choosy because I had a posh apartment. Going back in my condition was worse than starting again at the bottom of the ladder. It was the absolute gutter. I had a heroin habit that had to be fed. I started working the square and it was horrific because I was sick going to work. I'd no money to get any heroin and I had to find it no matter how I felt. I'd be with customers and the sweat would be pouring out of me. I had to work cars and I was very conscious of the fact that after working all those years to get girls out of that situation, there I was worse off than they were.

I told my cousin that I had to get a flat because, working on the streets, I really needed a place. Eventually he helped with the money for me to get a pad. I found a comfortable little bedsit on Pembroke Place. Though most of the time he was off doing his own thing, he still kept popping in and out of my life because he'd spend many a night in the apartment. My habit was still very high so I'd go out on the street at six in the evening. Occasionally I'd ask him to lend me ten or twenty pounds to get something. Sometimes he wouldn't, sometimes he would; he really had me begging.

The stuff was easy to get if you had the cash. It was everywhere; in certain areas there'd be ten or twelve people selling in the one street. In time I built up a great clientèle again, so sometimes I didn't have to go out. Street work was hard. I noticed the guards had become much more active. They were simply putting the girls away. I had to find the rent and the money for the stuff. Often I couldn't work because of the cops and because I needed stuff badly. The rent went up and up and up and eventually I was evicted. If it hadn't been for the guards I could have worked all night until I got the rent money.

The girls who had their pitches there were very tough too. I'd stand on the corner of Pembroke Place and Fitzwilliam Square and it was literally like being thrown into a pack of wolves. They were like animals and this was their territory but there was no way I was going to give into them. They obviously though I was some green new girl coming on the street. A few of them knew me at least by reputation though I didn't know them. A lot of them were English girls. The cheek of them! I said, 'You're coming over here telling me I can't work here on my own streets.' So I didn't give in. There were a couple of girls who, when they saw I wasn't going to yield, started blackmailing and threatening me.

I held out even though there were a few dodgy men around. If I thought there was any danger I'd go into the flats or disappear. It could be frightening, though, and looking back I realise it was probably the worst time of my life. My old pitch in Waterloo Road had gone downhill. The first time I was there it was known as one of the classy streets. There was Benburb Street and Waterloo Road and they were opposite extremes. When I worked there in the old days there were no girls except my friend and I. Then the odd new girl started coming out when they saw I could survive, but they were nice. By the time I was leaving the street things were getting nasty. There were heavies coming in, girls and customers being attacked; the place had gone downhill a lot.

I chose Fitzwilliam Square as it was more classy and had a better reputation. A lot of foreign customers would go there rather than Waterloo Road. It was new to me as well. I don't usually go back and cover old ground; that's not my habit. But I had girls threatening me: 'Marese O'Shea, we'll get you.' There was this one girl who had it in for me. I think she was so bitter because I wouldn't act as her agent one time. Now I know why I didn't take her on.

That was how I spent most of a year. I was still on heroin and then I gained a £200-a-day coke habit as well. It wasn't quite as dear as the heroin but it meant that I had to earn about £450 just to get through the day. It meant that there was no money for the rent or even for ordinary living. I never had money at home and I owed loads of people money. Since I've got clean, I've gone to people and said, 'I owe you money.' The amounts weren't huge: £10 or £20. There might have been one £50 but it was usually just tenners, bounced off everybody. I never forget a penny I owe anyone. It's just the way I've been all my life and I'm never happy until I've paid loans back. It feels really good when I meet people and I say, 'I owe you money'; it's a great feeling.

Matters about the flat got very bad. I had got heavily into Ecstasy as well. I realised I had to get off the heroin and the only way I knew how was to go away to get help. I always found that one of the hardest parts was trying to stay clean long enough to get into a place like Coolmine. You're out there on the streets, you don't know how to change your habits or how to cope emotionally. You go in for counselling every day or every second day and then you're back out again. The only hope is to try to lock yourself in.

18

COOLMINE

I lost the flat for not paying the rent but a couple of months before that I had made up my mind: I was very lonely with the habit and I wasn't seeing my cousin and I decided I was going to get off this drug. I was going to go back to Coolmine. I went in to see the counsellors in induction and they encouraged me. I worked on the street, still taking my heroin, but this time I had an aim. I worked till five or six in the morning every single night for a couple of weeks and I got a little money, enough to go on a two-week holiday with Catherine, because I knew I could get clean if I went away. I found it very hard to get clean; you have to get away from the people you know and your normal surroundings. Staying away is the secret. So by working twelve hours a night, I made enough to see the local travel agents and get fixed up with a holiday. I went to Formentera, a small island off Ibiza. It is really beautiful. You might almost be in the Caribbean. I used to spend all my time on the boats, on the water. I used no buses or cars, only ferries, and I spent every day out on the ocean.

My only company was Catherine. I wanted to spend some time alone with her and I knew that with her there I'd make an extra effort to keep clean. I drank quite a lot, took some methadone, smoked hash. I downed a couple of Es too while I was there – but no heroin! I was finding it very difficult, struggling in the morning to get out of bed, struggling to wash. But I had to make the effort for Catherine's sake and it was good for me. I came home determined not to see my cousin. I also found I was starting to become dependent on E and found myself calling to a drug dealer in the city looking for tablets every day. Every night I had to have E, so I cut them out too. Finally I started going to Coolmine; I got off everything eventually but it was hard.

I went into Coolmine on 1 September 1995 and came out in March the following year. That was six months, and I left only because my mother was dying. I'd been going to induction for a month. I was clean for a couple of weeks before I went in but I was still drinking. Things had got very bad at the house. My mother was very sick even before I went into Coolmine but I didn't know; all I knew was that she was very irritable. My daughter cracked up; she couldn't cope with me any more. It was she who helped save my life by saying to me, 'Look at you, you look like you have Aids you're so thin.' I was just skin and bone. I do have physical problems due to taking drugs, fortunately not Aids. Things got really bad at home so I had to escape. My daughter was freaking; she couldn't take it any more. She didn't believe me, naturally, because I had become such a liar when I was on heroin although I was trying to say, 'I am going to Coolmine.' A lot of people couldn't believe me but I had friends who supported me. Relatives and friends would give me the odd fiver but my very good old friend, Stephen, saved my life by financially supporting me so that I didn't go back to drugs and prostitution. A fiver a day sometimes saved my life; it was just enough for cigarettes.

Things had got so bad on the drugs and my life was so horrible that there is a lot I can't yet speak about. My daughter was going crazy and she was so angry that she became really violent. She wanted to smash things and I couldn't take it. I went out and injected heroin and that time I was so close to killing myself! I'd been off it for about five weeks but that day I couldn't take any more. I knew that if I couldn't get into Coolmine that week I was going to die. It was getting harder as the minutes went on to stay clean. You need support and I didn't have it. So as usual I went out and took drugs and as usual the counsellors in Coolmine were wonderful. They skilfully and tactfully put things right and I was back on track. A week and a half later I was back in Coolmine again.

Getting off drugs is no picnic. The use of substitutes, although it makes withdrawal easier, only delays the final detox. You've got to go through the sickness because you've taken drugs and the use of another drug as a substitute is only going to prolong things. That's why I think it's a bad idea in the long run to use methadone so much. People strung out on drugs or alcohol *can* get off them by doing it their own way, say by reducing their intake. OK sometimes, indeed often, they're so sick they need sedatives. But it has been proven by places like Coolmine that you don't need substitutes to come down off drugs.

I started going to induction in Coolmine hooked on heroin, cocaine, Ecstasy and hash, and within a week I had nothing. Everyone goes into a depression after coming down off drugs but all you need is friends and professional help of the kind given by the people in Coolmine to snap you out of it. It's no good having someone to come along and say, 'Poor you!' and let you wallow in misery. The system in Coolmine is based on self-help groups. Women, it seems to me, definitely need more personal help. The people in charge in Pearse Street came to talk to us and we told them that this daily attendance at their clinic was really pointless. Addicts were going there just to feed their habit or to get their physeptone and sell it. Methadone for three weeks solves nothing, and going into town for urine tests is a waste of time. I knew if I went that way I'd end up back on drugs again.

Every heroin addict abuses methadone. I got methadone a hundred times, bought it on the black market from people who could find a doctor who'd give them a bottle. I'd buy, say, two or three hundred millilitres and I'd have it there and say, 'I'll start taking that in measured doses.' I'd start taking thirty millilitres at a time but I ended up drinking the whole thing to get a buzz off it. It didn't work for me. Other people have to work out their own programmes but I still think that giving out doses of methadone is not really helping people. The only way is drug-free; you don't die from cold turkey. I'm proof of that. Nobody dies from kicking drugs. It's awful for a long, long time and then it starts getting better. But you do die from drugs, and methadone itself is one hell of a killer. Over a long period it has a very serious effect on your organs. Methadone is synthetic; it's just another evil. It does the same thing as heroin, and soothing the withdrawal from heroin is not in the end going to help the addict.

After a certain time in a place like Coolmine you feel ready to risk weekends at home. You have real friends in Coolmine, your peers, the ones who know the situation. You discuss it and listen to their advice. They may say, 'Well, I don't think you should.' The system helps you to open up. It really teaches you as if you were a child learning to understand your needs and your wants. For example, you can have a cup of tea only at certain times of the day and this makes you really appreciate being able to have a cup of tea any time you feel like it. They also have rules about cigarettes: you can't smoke at night. I used to keep breaking this rule, coming down during the night to have a cigarette. When I told them this I learned how everybody suffered in the house because of my behaviour, something I hadn't realised. Chocolate became a luxury. You'd get it only once a week. They don't allow biscuits or lemonade. These become a substitute for your real cravings. I used to come down during the night and eat cornflakes and that was stopped because I was substituting them too. I got very annoyed over the cornflakes but it was through experiences like that that I learned how to take care of myself. I owe my life to Coolmine.

My period of residence in Coolmine was what brought about the lasting change in me. There were fifteen or twenty women and we began our day at 7.15 am. We had breakfast and then cleaned up the house. Then there might be a meeting or you would go for a walk – there was always activity. We all had jobs to do which we volunteered for at the monthly business meeting. We made our own decisions on the self-help principle. We'd have counselling sessions every day, in groups and individually. We'd have Narcotics Anonymous meetings, dental or hospital appointments, generally a full day and a very active life. It might sound like a prison but I don't think it was one; I've never been in prison so I don't know what it's like. I suppose it's a prison in your mind. We weren't kept locked up; the doors were always open.

I had never kept rules in my life and when you don't live by rules everybody else is affected. That is one of the most important things you learn there. Coolmine taught me an awful lot about myself, stuff I wasn't aware of. Now my awareness of the world is much improved, as is my awareness of myself. There were assertiveness courses and debates. The people there made sure that we had our fun needs met every day. We'd play games and we were allowed to watch television. Sometimes we would have 'closed houses' where nobody was allowed to leave the house and it was solid work all day, no radio, no television. That would go on for a few weeks and it was hard. The closed house system was a kind of punishment for inappropriate behaviour.

The staff would come in and ask us: 'What do you feel? How do you think it should be handled?' It was for us to make the decisions. There were two psychotherapists and they would talk to us and point out certain things about our behaviour to make us understand what the consequences of our decisions might be. Some of them had done drugs themselves and I think addicts like me will give more and respond better to someone who really understands. When they know that the counsellors have been in the same difficulties as themselves they believe them, trust them, and wouldn't think of lying to them.

I remember seeing a psychiatrist when I was younger and he hadn't a clue what I was going through. In the psychotherapy sessions in Coolmine it was great. You felt that the people had been exactly where you were; they knew how you were feeling and thinking. Eventually in the group sessions the addicts were able to take charge themselves. You began to see the games people were playing because you'd played them yourself. The group would consider what we thought was good for one another and what wasn't. Everybody in the house took part. We had every single person there because the decisions that we made affected us all; everyone had to have an input.

I class Coolmine as totally different from everything that had happened in my life up to then. It was there that I formed lasting attachments for the first time. It was the only time I've felt real. I've tried to be very honest about myself doing this book and it's probably very good for me to do it so soon after Coolmine. A lot of stuff has resurfaced that I was pushing down, blocking out. I'm still dealing with it. In Coolmine no day is a pain; it's an amazing place; it's wonderful. For the first time in my life I had a home and I made real friends. Initially it was in very bad nick; they need donations very badly. When the new staff came they had the whole house done up. We did most of the actual work and it's very comfortable, really very pleasant. I used to laugh so much with the other girls up in our bedrooms, an experience I'd never had before. It was a bit like a boarding school you'd read about. I never had a sister but I felt sisterly with the women there.

Some of the women I knew are still there. I go to the induction centre to keep in touch with myself. One of the people I knew there has since died of an overdose. She was only twenty-two and she really was fighting very hard, but she left. She wanted drugs and she was found dead soon afterwards. It happens quite a lot when people leave Coolmine: their awareness of themselves is so improved that when they *do* go back on drugs they know the road they're on. They really don't want to go back on it and I suppose death is a brighter outlook once and for all. I think there is a lack of self-confidence as well; you feel as if you can't do it. Yet I firmly believe that everybody *can* do it, and I'd been taking drugs for two decades, ever since I was fifteen.

19

LOOKING TO THE FUTURE

Writing this book has cost me a great deal. I feel I've gone through hell. People I know keep trying to stop me, asking if I'm mad. What they mean is: 'You're better off going out and working as a prostitute than doing this.' I do have one friend who has stood by me through it all. He said, 'Go and do what you feel you have to do.' I'm not asking anybody to be proud of me but I'm sick and tired of this hiding all the time, this deceit. When people, especially prostitutes, hide things from themselves as well as from other people they are on the road to nowhere. That is why people are ending up strung out on drugs or even dead. It was right enough for me to do it and make a living out of it so it's right enough for me to come out and say to people, 'This is me!'

The money I got as an advance for this book was the first legal money I had earned in eighteen years and it felt really good. I put it towards my psychotherapy course. I am thirty-six and in those years I've faced a lot of things. I can't block out completely things like the bone disease I got after my early menopause and the effect it has had on my mobility. I have to face the possibility that I'm going to need a wheelchair eventually.

On the brighter side I have started the psychotherapy course which will, I hope, lead to a diploma. I go to lectures one night a week and at weekends. It leaves me time for other things. In the meantime I've no home to go to. One of my priorities is to prepare myself to get my home together. I always thought I had a home but my mother left it in her will to my daughter. I also have to find a way of making a living.

To be honest, it's very hard to let the escort business go because I know I'm still good at it. I'm aware that madness and sleaziness are still part of prostitution but my original motive in starting the agency was to make it safe and clean, and that still seems to me a good thing to do. Human appetites are not going to change and the need for a properly organised system such as I had is as great as ever. Two weeks after I re-opened, the phone was hopping with girls and customers wanting me back again. In one way I feel it's wrong to turn my back on it as I'm doing. I feel I'm just walking away from a problem I can help to solve, and perhaps my work there isn't finished yet.

I'm very angry at society for the way prostitutes are treated. Prostitution in itself is not wrong – it's a contract between two consenting adults, one providing a service, the other paying for it. It's a form of entertainment and doesn't have to damage people's lives – after all many of the customers are not married. The oldest profession in the world is never going to go away so it should be recognised. The bad things that are associated with it – abuse of prostitutes by customers and brothel-owners;

blackmailing of customers; theft from customers – all these thrive in the climate of illegality and would be much easier to control if prostitution were legal and properly regulated. I believe that women in all walks of life perform sexual services on a casual or regular basis – sometimes in return for nothing more than a bottle of wine. But other women are respected; prostitutes are despised and treated as if they have no feelings at all. It is a human right to choose prostitution as a career and gain the same respect for it as you would for any other career. At the moment it is only the prostitutes themselves who regulate the business – for instance by discouraging girls who are too young from going into it – and I'm really angry at the way legislators refuse to face up to their responsibilty to change the law. When I see photos in newspapers of politicians who are former clients of mine it makes me seethe with anger to know that these pillars of society who used my service as if it were legal would deny me completely as a person. I think of the words of President Mary Robinson: 'In a society where the rights and potential of women are constrained, no man can be truly free. He may have power but he will now have freedom.'

Why then am I reluctant when I truly believe that the escort work needs to be done and that I am specially gifted in it? One reason is that it's just so demanding. It becomes so powerful; it begins to dominate me. It's very hard for me to draw the line and say, 'That's it. I'm not taking on any more.' It just takes over my life and becomes so time-consuming that I've no time for me. I may have to stay away from it altogether to protect myself from going back on drugs. Before I would consider starting up again things would have to be very different. There are a few exclusive people out there whom I still look after as regards introductions. But if I went back into the business the publicity would be going full belt and everybody would be trying to get hold of me.

My biggest fear is of the pressure getting to me and my going straight back to drugs. I am a drug addict and I could find myself back using tomorrow. Going back into the agency would give me the excuse that I secretly want to take drugs again. Addicts become very devious in their yearning for their drug and play these crazy head-games with themselves. Yet I don't want to walk away from it. I can't because I've worked in this business all my life; it's what I know best. There *has* been a small change in attitudes but there's still a long way to go. The more girls who come out and say, 'We're here; we do a necessary job!' the faster change will take place. They're coming out, not just for themselves but for others who come after them. They might not want their own children to go into the same job but that doesn't mean that they're not going to. It could happen to anybody.

For my own part I've got an eighteen-year-old daughter with whom I am still involved. My mother had the main rearing of her, although I tried to keep in touch as much as I could. They moved house quite often, sometimes because of me. The publicity I got from time to time embarrassed my mother. She shifted regularly between the Navan Road and the south side of the city. This meant that Catherine's schooling was disrupted. I am not saying that some of the fault wasn't mine. My mother brought her up and I was glad that she still had the nursery school because it meant that Catherine had the company of other children. Yet I didn't desert her; I dropped in regularly and there wasn't a day that passed without my ringing her. As she got older my drug habit became stronger and I withdrew that bit more. The result is that my daughter is angry and I have to live with that. When I was in Coolmine my main reason for losing hope and and rejecting the programme was that I found it hard to live with the guilt and the hurt. I know that things can change and that at some future time Catherine might find it in her heart to forgive me.

Catherine misses my mother dreadfully; she was always with her, idolised her, looked after her. It was heartbreaking for her but she'll get strong; she'll get through. We did everything we could for my mother but her death was not easy. She was elderly by then and when I came out of Coolmine to nurse her in March 1996 she had an advanced case of cancer of the bowel. The morning she died my daughter called me down and said, 'Louise, she's breathing real funny.' She'd been in a coma for a few days and I said, 'I'll be down in a minute.' I thought everything was all right because she hadn't moved or changed but I had only arrived at the bed when she took her second-last breath Then she breathed her last. It was amazing; it was as if she had been waiting for me to come.

I nursed my mother full-time at the end, and she wasn't the first person I had nursed. A few years before her illness my daughter and I had nursed her brother Reggie, who also died of cancer. We took him home to our house for the last two weeks of his life and felt very lucky to have had him with us. But for some reason I've always found it very hard to look after myself. Even during the treatment, learning to look after myself was the hardest part because I have this need to give to everybody else. I'll tend to someone who's sick even if I am really in worse shape than they are. I'll give them my time before I give it to myself.

I would love to go back to Coolmine to 'graduate' but now does not seem to me to be the proper time. I'm hoping the psychotherapy course I'm doing will give me as much as I need now. The lectures and study are giving me the foundation. The result of the tests about my physical condition will help me to make a decision. I know without a doubt that living a drug-free life is the best thing I could ever hope for.

I have things to face: my biological family don't want to know me. Nothing new in that! I sent my mother a letter when I was in Coolmine letting her know that I realised how much I had hurt her and that I would be very grateful for an opportunity to meet her. She didn't respond, so when I came out, after my adoptive mother died, I contacted her by phone and asked her if we could meet some day for a coffee. I feel she didn't want to know. She just said, 'Yeah, maybe some day.' One of my sisters gave me a picture of her and her family and I keep it on my mantelpiece. I really do want to make contact. People can change and I'm prepared to make the effort.

I've tried to be very open about myself in this book. Over Christmas 1996 I struggled quite seriously with my life and drugs and I ended up going and getting heroin from one of the same dealers I was getting it from years back. He'd been moved out of an inner-city area but he had only moved half a mile down the road. He had been run off by the community but the same guy was still selling. It was as easy as a phone call to get in touch: just contact an addict and you're back in there. It's totally out of your control then.

One of the things that I considered were my reasons for revealing so much about myself in this book. One reason is that I am me, a real separate person, and by reading the book people may discover the life that I have led. Not every prostitute can be fitted into a category. I know that prostitutes are typecast and if this book helps in any way to dispel that prejudice it will be wonderful. Also, I'm tired of hiding. When I was a baby I was always hidden, always hiding. The first time I got in trouble with the papers was years ago, at the time of the court case about the Bay Tree. I was exposed to the public then. I did not want the publicity but from then on I knew I would go the whole hog. That's when I knew that I would take up prostitution as a career. I was going to use it. OK, I'd been exposed, exploited. It was done and there was nothing else they could do to me.

Perhaps the strongest motive for this self-exposure is to show that drug addiction can be fought and conquered. It worked for me; I'm here alive. I'm still battling with drugs but I'm clean. I'm off heroin now. Instead of sleeping my life away I'm beginning to enjoy living. When I saw hard drug addicts come down I would say to myself, 'If they can do it I can.' For so many addicts out there living is hell. I hope that when they read the book they say to themselves, 'If she can do it, so can I.'